Do Down

Horace Belvins Helmick

-1-

DO DOWN

The sign above her head read THE VENTURI EFFECT. The sign directly behind her, IMPOUNDED DARLENES. Two simple, orderly arrangements of words, sufficiently harmonious at most times of the day and night, I should think. But I take out my pen now and change those signs. I change IMPOUNDED DARLENES to LOVE AND RESPECT. And THE VENTURI EFFECT on the higher sign I replace with GET IT WHILE YOU CAN. Those aren't my sentiments. No, that's just what she looks like. That's what those signs would say if they had been designed for her.

I watch her every morning while she's waiting for her bus. I am the green deity up in a leafy tree across the broad street. I watch her straighten her golden socks. Gold? No, she is not money, not even with a blue-purple body would she be money. Light? Is she light? When that one small, flat area of white on the otherwise black-dark ground near my head where I sleep every night rises like a funnel and turns to greet me, then she will be light.

If she's not light now, how can I see her, you ask? I can't see her. I don't think I ever could (did). I know I said that "I watch her." But what I see, if anything, is not a *her* but the complete character of the divine shape. Form. And the promise of content. But only the promise of content.

Do I know her name? Of course I know her name. It's laid/written right over her clothes in a big, round, sky-blue hand, two dozen times all across and up and down her front and her sides and her back: Hossmattcha. Which I think translates to "Have a heart." I don't know what language it is. I'm saying I can read her name from clear across the boulevard.

Love and respect? I doubt it. She does look good, however, in whatever outfit she's wearing that day. Get it while you can? Naw, I don't think so. Not me anyway. That's just the way she looks, the way she stands there, the twist of a shoulder, the tilt of her head. Then I think…and it occurs to me that LOVE AND RESPECT and GET IT WHILE YOU CAN don't really go together. They seem to be working in opposite directions, don't they? Yet that's the way she looks, truly.

And how can that be? Maybe I don't understand the words, both the old words of the signs and my replacements for them. Most certainly I don't understand what the way she dresses means. Blank, blank, blank. Those last three words were meant to be heard in the same vein as one would hear "bang, bang, bang" in a cowboy/war/gangland movie. Or in the backroom of your local post office. Termination! Or at least the threat of termination. Or the hope of termination. Or the presence of termination. Or the mind of termination.

Dogs and cats running down the sidewalk behind her, literally hundreds of them dogs and cats. And the ninny that I am thinks that means something. What could it mean? Beats me? And she's always the only one to get on the bus. And the bus is empty, except for the driver, whose face I can never quite see.

But that was yesterday. Today, she didn't come to the corner, not yet anyway. According to the public clock on my side of the street, she is already twenty-five minutes late. And there's not a sign of her.

I'm just now realizing that her bus hasn't gone by either. Does that mean that I'm dead and nothing new can happen, ever again? Well, I guess there's no way to know that except to just wait and see.

When would I have died? When did the last new thing happen? No wait! That won't tell me if I'm alive or dead. It's possible that nothing new has ever happened.

I used to use—back when I had a shower—yellow shampoo and turquoise bodywash in hopes they would permanently change the colors of my hair and skin. I did eventually get the green skin, yes; and early on my hair turned sort of yellow during the sunny summer months, until each and every hair on my head and body too awoke spit-white one morning when I was just nineteen.

Black. . .

Well that didn't work! I was trying to use the word *black* the way I used the words *blank* and *bang* above. *Blue* would have been a better word in this case, because I wanted a color and pure black is often called "an absence of color," even though white is more logically an absence of color. I know that all the "artists" out there will want to argue that point. So I just say, "Blue, blue, blue to both of you."

See more. I say, see more. See more of the sea. See it firsthand. No beach, no dock, no boat. Just you and the sea. And then you'll see.

"Always becoming." Who first said that? To get any kind of useful answer wouldn't I have to clarify first whether I meant *who first said that in this language* or *who first said that in any language*? Maybe no, maybe not. Maybe I wouldn't have to bother with that distinction if I took the tack that a word is a word; hence, a translation of a word is not that word. Hence, I ask again, "Who first said that?" And the answer is necessarily me. No, it's not; it's you, because you *just* read it. You and not me? On down the line, I'm afraid, that won't make much if any sense. How much if any sense does it make now?

Bounce, bounce, bounce.

Whoo! There she is now! Hossmattcha!

And here comes the bus.

And what about the clock? How can that be? The clock says that it's just now time for the woman's appearance. And it's the right time for the bus too.

What did it say before, the clock? What did it say when I thought the woman and the bus were late? I'm sure that clock has already said today what it's saying right now.

Why do I have to discipline myself? Why isn't this machine built to run at optimum speed right out of the chute? If I want to partake in the unsoiled pleasures available to humans I have to spend years rigorously training my body and mind, and that doesn't seem reasonable at all. Of course the aging process does most of the work for us. We just have to not be so greedy/stupid/etc. But that's not easy. Not at all.

Did you hear me doing that *we* stuff? Gives me the shivers. Next I'll be climbing down from this tree and trotting over there to catch a bus myself. Gag!

Double gag!

Keep all your dogs in a row.

Or would that be "Keep all your dogs in a room"?

In a row, I think. I could do a saying for cats too, couldn't I? Nope, that would lead me in short order to giraffes on the moon, an obvious dead end. But aren't all dead ends merely new beginnings? Ugh! That one outright stunk of nice-guyness. Got to keep my chin off my chest. Which leads me in short order to another dead end: Who's chest could I keep my chin on? A question like that shouldn't exist anywhere in the universe. Yet there it is in the second sentence back.

Sun.

I said *sun* because I was thinking about water, just like I just said *water* because I'm now thinking about the sun. I'm thinking about the sun. Think about the sun! Think about the sun!

She's getting on the bus. Again, there is no one already on the bus other than the driver. She's sitting down on her regular seat—next to the window, second row back from the front, across the aisle from the driver—and spreading her things on the seat beside her.

I never paid much mind to other people's fantasies. My own were so much more valid. There is no line on earth that goes straight to where it seems to be going.

There are two words, *car* and *notes*, that someone before me carved into the bark of this tree. "Before me?" Sounds like history, huh? I don't know what to make of the words. I've never had a car, and I never take notes. Notes about what? What's written down is not what was or will be or anything except what's written down. Another false promise of a more interesting life.

I rest my forehead against the trunk of the tree so that my right eye is blocked from seeing anything but the word *car* and the tree's bark right around the word. So I close that eye. Out the other eye I see a more or less vertical line. To the right of the line, I have a close-up of dark bark. To the left of the line, a clear shot of the bus pulling away from the curb. The bus, all bright and shiny, glass and enamel. Green and blue and beige. What kind of word is *beige*? It smells like it is of Persian origin. Wow! That was easy enough to say right off the top of my head. Or right off the top of the swimming pool that's my mind.

Yep, it's *dogs in a row.* That other choice, *dogs in a room*, doesn't make any sense for people like me.

"…people like me." I'm quoting myself. Now I know I shouldn't have said something like that, but I did. I did say it, and what did I mean?

Let's try an obvious answer first. *People like me* speaks of categories, trees compared to fences. That was easy enough to say right off the top of our linguistic conditioning. It was, however, unmistakably unsatisfactory. No taste, no grit. Next we will try a tricky answer. People *like* me. No, even if that were true, evasion is not going to be tolerated here.

There is me and everyone whom I could consider to be under my influence. (Hah! Maybe I don't necessarily have to have ever met any of these people.) And then there is the not-like-me, everyone else.

Was that bucket of dunk any less obvious or of any more use than my first attempt, the intentionally obvious answer? I'm sure not. I seem to be making no progress in explaining what I meant. I must be blocking any serious attempt to understand my questionable statement. I'll pretend to forget the problem for now. It wasn't of any considerable weight anyhow.

Buses blow stink. Babies cry. How will your life end? Or is it going to go on forever, like mine has? I once knew a woman who understood what I meant when I talked like that. She didn't immediately yell at me that no one lives forever. What she did was kind of grin out the corner of her mouth and then whistle one soft swooping note. I knew she understood.

Her understanding did me little good, though. She never said anything, never spoke a word. She was a comfort in the night and a hard worker in the daylight. But we never talked. I occasionally spat out some crazy thing like the above and she grinned and whistled, and that was the day's conversation. Just like that. Nothing more, nothing less. That's when I knew my life would go on forever.

A battered truck is coming down the street, looking exactly like a ragged, worn-down boot. I think I saw that image in a comic strip somewhere. I don't remember the story that went with the truck. Maybe I should make one up. OK. Let me tell you a story.

Who am I kidding? I don't have any stories to tell. My life is as empty of content (do you remember my speaking about the divine shape, "But only the promise of content"?) as yours undoubtedly is.

Maybe that's the big gear that's always eating people to death. I once knew a guy who was always talking about this giant gear in the sky. I didn't have any idea then what he was talking about. I thought he had a hole in his head other than the hole he was talking through. Maybe lack of content was/is this gear. Now that I've maybe popped through, I suppose I'll be hearing people being eaten by the gear all night every night. "Reminds me of you."

I can't remember any other words of that song.

"Moving into water." That's from something, too. I don't think it was a song, though. Maybe it was a painting, back when people looked at paintings. I think it was in a museum. Or in someone's dining room. Of course it could have been just three random words on the wall above a filthy urinal, three words scratched at eye-level into the metal by three different people on three different days...and these three words hooked together in my brain to form a mythic trinity. Moving into water? What is moving? And whatever is moving, is it moving into water like walking into a lake? Or is it moving into *becoming* water, *turning into* water. Or, backing up, maybe there is no subject preceding the action-word *moving*.

Chaos into cosmos or cosmos into chaos? I ask that about my brainee all the time. Or would that be my mind? Am I characteristic of the world? It's still possible that the only thing wrong with me is that I've got brain fag. That's mental fatigue, in case you've never heard the two words used together. *Together* is a strange word. To...get...her. How did that become two or more people/things in the same spot at the same time with a feeling/illusion of unity? Beats me upside the head.

Ah! The now tiny bus is down at the end of the last block in which I can still see it. It's turning the corner. It's gone.

It will be back in an hour or so, but Hossmattcha

won't be on it. I won't see her again today. I have no idea how she gets back here from wherever she is going. Or is that an upsidedown way of looking at it? It's possible that she resides where she's going right now, and somewhere around here is where she goes out to every day. But I doubt that because she looks so nice and fresh every morning when I see her over there.

Do I have sex-thoughts about her?

That was not a facetious question. Yes, it sounded like one. It wasn't.

I could be having sex-thoughts about her right now and not know it. Brain fag, remember? Somewhere over there behind that blue-grey fog might be me appreciating Hossmattcha's many physical charms in blazing fleshy colors, whatever colors are fleshy at the moment. I might be reaching out for her. I might already have her clutched tightly to me.

Of course I can't see anything like that, but it's possible.

Do I wish I could see something like that?

Wouldn't such a wish be closer to me and therefore more visible than possibly submerged sex-thoughts? Still, I cannot see the wish. Yes or no, I would have to simply guess. And when you guess it's no longer a wish. So I would have to say, no, I don't wish I could see something like that.

I've thought about it for a while now, and the wish still has not taken form in any place I can see.

It's morning again. Still too dark to tell blue from green. It must be...what month? Or have they-out-there changed the months too to save time? Or is it light that they're trying to save? I use the sun to tell time, not some watch that I could change to tell whatever time I want it to, regardless of where the sun is. Foolishness.

Obviously I'm the one who is a fool, sitting up here in a tree. Near the corner of 6th and Page. Wearing whose body? Wearing what body? Is my thinking today going to be limited to what's right in front of my eyes? If I could see the sea, then I would see.

Forms and feelings. Mind and matter. Names and numbers.

Didn't we talk yesterday about notes, taking notes? If you record everything that happens to you for your whole life and then you sort through all these records, sorting by time or emotional load or the first letter of the entry or by any *by*, how could your life turn out to be any brighter, clearer, or more valuable to you than if you had just sat and carefully watched? Like I do, you ask? Am I another salesman trying to convince you to try another lifestyle? Nope. That's not me. So why did I reintroduce note-talking, you ask? Beats me, again and again. I can't seem to figure out any of the obviously many reasons why things come to mind. But one thing that I do know... No, I'd better not say *know*; that may be overstatement. One thing that *appears* to me is that if I let things come and go naturally, not bothering to correct anything no matter how silly it is, everything works out just fine and I can look back and see that there were no mistakes made. Of course you'll ask then what happens when I look at the present or into the future. Does my having seen that no mistakes have been made in the past make my living in the present any easier? Is my tolerance of how I'm acting right now upped? Yes, no, certainly, not a bit. The future? I'd rather not talk about the future right now. Hey! "The future right now." An interesting word combination.

Speaking of words, I'm thinking about the word *mistake* that I just used. (I sort of used the word yesterday too while I was trying to explain my people-like-me statement, when I said, "...*unmistakably unsatisfactory*.") It's surely of no consequence at this late date, yet I'm curious. Original-meaningwise, is it *miss-take*, or is it *my-stake*? Hah! An uncalled-for rasher of dark humor there. If you didn't get it, I apologize. Sorry. Morry. Torry.

And here comes Hossmattcha. In the first clear light. Everything is sharp. Things aren't bright yet, but they're sharp. Clear and sharp. Is that a redundant statement? I won't worry about it right now. Here comes Hossmattcha.

"Hi, Hoss."

I know there are quotes around that, but I did not cry out to her. I merely thought that greeting. *Hi, Hoss.* She doesn't know I'm here. Or have I already said that? At least I assume she's not aware I'm up in this tree watching her every morning. But—hey!—she could well have spotted me right off and has just been ignoring me ever since.

Why did I say *ignoring me*? Do I like to beat up on myself? No way. Hossmattcha clearly has not been posturing for me. So that leaves (1) *ignoring me* and (2) *not knowing I'm here*. Doesn't it? Yes, yes, there's *indifferent to me* too, but I meant that to be included in *ignoring me*.

What's that? I'm hearing a high, shrill voice. Male or female? "...we're family and we're not going to tolerate being separated..." Hmm. Don't know where that came from. Up the street or down? Or it could even have come from behind me. It's hard to tell the directions of sounds from up in this tree.

Yes, yes, there's also *interested but disciplined*. I could always fantasize that's she's very much interested in me but too well-mannered to show herself to me. Boy! Wouldn't that be a waste of time. No one is interested in me. And to tell the truth, I'm not interested in them either, not in any one person, not even Hossmattcha, not in that way anyway. I'll quote myself from yesterday: "But what I see, if anything, is not a *her* but the complete character of the divine shape." I'm bringing up the rear in this culture. In fact, I am so far to the rear that I don't even know if there still *is* a functioning culture. There must be. The last time I heard any talk about that sort of thing, people were saying that people could not exist for any length of time without producing a well defined culture for themselves. That seemed like a debatable point then, but now I'm not even interested. Culture—in fact, I'll go all the way and say civilization—is way way down on my list. No, that does not mean that I am an unrestrained, potentially violent person. I'm just "out of the loop."

Today, I think the sign above her head should read INTELLECTUAL AND ARTISTIC CONTENT.

Hmm. I can't come up with something new for the sign behind her. I'll forget it for now. Oops! Wait! The sign behind her could read SET GENERAL CONTROL. Yes'um.

She has on those gold socks again. She doesn't wear them every day, just most days. Like I've said before, I don't understand the way she dresses. That is not to imply that I do understand how someone else in this world dresses.

When it comes to knowledge of dressing, my bank is blank.

Is she looking at me? Naw. She may be looking at the tree, but she's not looking at me. People don't look at other people like that. That's a looking-at-pleasant-scenery look.

She's turning her head to look down the street. With good reason. Here comes the bus.

There is not a thought in my head, except this one.

And now there are thoughts all over the place. Yet not one of them fixes firmly enough to be remembered. Nope, not true, here is one: *I cling to life as dearly as anyone, but I am not really all that sure that life is worth that much trouble.*

Is it true? Do I really feel that way? (I am asking myself. And I know I sound vapid.) Maybe all this ingestion and ejaculation of stupid energy has a point that I've missed so far. Every *thing*, every idea (also a thing) is undeniably empty. But is *empty* synonymous with *pointless*? That last question promptly flopped on its side like a dog. No, like a cat I once knew. Should I pick up the question, sit it upright on its feet, and order it to chase its tail round and round endlessly trying to find an answer for me. (Now that was a terrible sentence, warped every which way. I could have just as easily said, "Meet my mother.")

And Hoss is getting on the bus and the bus is empty and the driver's face is not seeable. So what's new.

So what's new? I'm asking a question this time. So what's new?

Elapsed time.

Elapsed time is not a new concept. I'm positive of that. Yet in a way it is new to me. Can you feel into what I am saying? Elapsed time. What do those two words stand for? Whatever elapsed time is, it's very subtle. Where does it begin? Where does it end? And the stuff in the middle: How could there be anything there but a jumble?

Excuse me a second, please, while I tune up the reds.

There. That's right now.

She's sitting her things on the seat beside her. Yeah, and the driver is probably saying something to her, like "Good morning." Or would it be "Good morning, Hossmattcha"? Can he—it could be a she, couldn't it? Can the driver see Hossmattcha's name written all over her clothes? Truthfully, I don't see her name anymore. I used to, every morning. Or does the driver know Hoss as an individual? It's possible. I say to the both of them as the bus starts rolling, "Straighten up and fly right." Do I know what that means? Not really. I've heard it before, though. When, where and why I heard it, I don't know or care to know. My saying that I don't care to know probably means that I heard it in an unpleasant situation.

Metal Mouse. Or Mighty Metal Mouse. Or Mighty Metal Mass-Transit Mouse. I'm trying to make up a name for the bus. The *mouse* might not be right. Mice don't carry passengers. Back off! That's not true. They supposedly pack around many many little critters. So *mouse* is all right. And *metal* is all right. But *mighty*, when hooked so close to *mouse*, might cause problems. Let's try *Metal Mass-Transit Mouse.* Nope. That sounds dingy. Let's forget the whole thing and keep on just calling it *the bus.*

The bus. The bus. It's going around the corner…and it's gone. Another viewing of Hossmattcha gone and done with. PRUYTGVS.

+

What's that? Is it that shrill voice from this morning again? No…it's not. Yes, I'm right; it's definitely not the same voice. (That would have been spooky, having the irritating voice that I heard from up in the tree follow me here. That would have been definitely spooky.) And this voice here is not crying out in desperation, like the one this morning was; this voice is—was laughing. It did not sound like it was laughing in good humor, though. Yet it did not sound unashamedly desperate either. The laugh wasn't *just* a laugh. I think it came from immediately over the top of that hill over there. It wasn't a simple laugh: it was a loaded laugh.

I close my eyes. I can hear the ducks and geese and frogs and various insects on the pond. I'm lying on my back now, and if my outstretched left arm were twice as long as it is, I could touch the edge of the pond. The grass hasn't been mowed in a while; it's tall enough to find its way into my ears.

I open my eyes. The sun is high; it's a little past the real noon of this day. My body temperature feels normal and stable; in other words, the earth's not sucking the heat out of me. A bit of breeze can be seen up in the tops of the trees. I see one…two…three birds in the sky. I see one…two…three…four manmade flying contraptions in the sky. I see one…two elongated clouds in the sky. I see blue in the sky. I see long, curving black lines in the sky. I see a faint moon in the sky. I can sort of see stars in the sky, but that might be just the back inside of my eyeballs acting up, my own little lightshow.

I saw the insides of my eyeballs once. I was standing looking at a mirror that someone had fixed to the inside of a shop window. The sunlight was just right, and I saw into my eyes—I could actually see through some clear stuff all the way to the back of my eyeballs. The experience was like visiting another world for ten seconds.

I am remembering that I once met a woman here on this spot on the grass. I knew at the time that before we did anything of consequence she would say she did not know what she was doing. No, that's not quite right; that's not what I knew ahead of time. She would not say that she did not know what she was doing; what she would say was that she did not know she was doing what anyone else (me in particular) would think she was doing if they or I watched (witnessed) what she was doing. What did *she* think she was doing, I imprudently asked after she had indeed made this claim. "Nuthing." She, she said, did not think she was doing anything. At the time I could only translate that to mean she wasn't thinking at all. Moving ahead in time a little, on a couple of occasions after that day, when I asked her (the same woman) what she thought she was doing, she promptly said each and every time that she did not think she was doing anything. Was she the perfect, uninvolved perceptor? I doubt it.

Arousing or suited or designed to arouse a quick, intense, and usually superficial emotional response. Now, that's a good definition for something. What would this something be? I shall think on that. And I'll think without resorting to a search of my memory to find where I got that grouping of words, for certainly they are not just a random assembly.

Aye. And aye again. I thunk about it. While there may be many things that could use those words as their definition, I only came up with one thing that seemed to me to fit, another word, *sensational.* It fits righteously.

As I dragged *sensational* through my does-it-fit sieve, another question, general and academic, seemingly unrelated, popped up. Did time erase the magic, or did time turn the things that could no longer happen after time had happened into magic, or did magic invent time? Sounds like a waste of time to me. No pun intended. No pun achieved. Let it go.

The hearer on the ground hears something. I think someone is coming up behind me. How could anyone be *behind* me while I'm laying on my back? So many words are based on the idea that the *normal* position of a person is vertical, up and down, on their feet, aligned with gravity. So what should I say? I think someone is coming up *above* me? Sounds ridiculous, huh?

Sounds more like two people. Are they going to walk right over me, smear my face with their big shoes? I've got my eyeballs rolled to their limits, as if I'm trying to see a biting fly on my forehead. Don't see anyone yet.

Ah! They walk up and stand one on each side of me. Police? No. Someone I know? No. Someone I've at least seen before? Yes. One of them I've seen before. Not the other one.

The one that I've seen is a woman. The other, a man. The woman was sitting alone on the old iron-and-wood bench just outside the zoo fence a few days ago, wearing a lime-green dress and yellow shoes. Actually, now that I think about it, I've seen her sitting there on that bench several times, wearing completely different clothes and a different hairstyle every time. But those sightings were all a while ago. I have not seen her recently. Zole is her name. It's written in thumbprints (not fly bites) around her calf.

Zow! She just sent me a flash, a friendly letter, a smile.

"How are you…"

I got her first three words, but then what she was saying turned into garble. I'm gawking up at her. She's grinning down at me. What's the guy doing? He's standing there silently on the other side of me with his hands in his pockets and his feet apart. Am I required by public law to stand up now, too? Must I climb to my feet or face the guillotine? Where—*how* would I find the quintessential instruction for what to do in this situation? Mine seems like a common enough predicament that there must be an instruction available somewhere that would help me avoid breaking whatever law applies here. Did I hear a cry for common decency echoing from the back pew? It's coming down to snip and snap, is it? OK, OK, OK. I'll stand up.

Wow! How come I'm three feet taller than either of them? I haven't been this close to anyone in a while, but three feet taller…?

I close my eyes and turn clear around in a circle. Good! The proportions straightened right out. I had locked into some kind of faraway perspective (from lying so long on my back?) and had a god-like view of this part of the world. Do I suffer delusions of omnipotence? No, not in any way, though I may suffer slightly from periodic delusions of solitariness.

Which one should I face? I can't face both of them. I'll face away so that they will again be one on either side of me. Then *they* will have to decide where they are going to stand.

The woman is inching around so that she can see my face. The guy seems satisfied to just stare at my profile. This must be what it feels like to be a beautiful green-glass vase in a museum.

Can they see that I am green?

I can see more than her smile on the woman's face now. She has sky-blue eyes and paler-than-ivory skin with orange freckles. Fine lines show around her eyes and the corners of her mouth. Her lips are almost as lightly colored as her skin. Her hair? It's so fine and pale it can hardly be seen, especially her eyebrows, which are all but invisible. The only things clearly colored on her head are her freckles. They are very distinct.

When I saw this woman sitting on the bench over by the zoo, more than once, she was not so blond that she's almost transparent. Which means what? Obviously this isn't the same woman. I've never seen this woman before. Why did I think I had?

I can smell her. No, the smell is something she put on herself. What—?

The man had taken my hand. He's shaking it now. He's saying something. I can't hear him. Short, dark hair, precisely combed. Yellow-brown skin, with a half-dozen tiny scars on his neck. He is not looking me in the eye. Is he afraid of me? He may be afraid of something, but it's not me.

Oh, the keen incongruity of this couple. They are an unmatching set; they don't go together at all. Then I realize that their incongruity may exist only in my wrong first-impression of them. These two could be a pair of identical sharpies. If that be the case, however, what do they want from me? What do I have that they don't already have? Beats me again and again and again.

Am I coming on with attitude even before I have spoken?

Am I going to be able to speak?

What would I talk about? I could mention the length of the grass, the sound that the baby ducks make, the new cloud that's forming over on the western horizon. But more likely I will be required to talk about whatever brought them to me. Which I don't know what that is. Not yet. I am deciding right now to assume that I will eventually learn why they came to me.

The fellow has a book in his other hand, an expensively bound book. What's that title? Reading upsidedown… "Mental Pliancy Is A Factor Of Lightness." Hmm. I've seen that sentence somewhere before, but it wasn't the title of a book. So I ask the man what is the first line of that book you're carrying.

He pretends he didn't know he was packing a book. Then he recognizes the book in his hand and opens it and turns to the first page of the body of the book.

He looks surprised by what he's seeing there. "The first line reads," he says in probably the deepest voice he can muster without sounding like a complete bumpkin, "'Beauty is not empty. Life may be empty, but Beauty is not.'"

I mumble back to him that that sounds like an indefensible statement if I ever heard one.

"You bet!" he says. "I wholeheartedly agree." He turns a few pages, as if he is looking for something. "Obviously this isn't the same book. I've never seen this book before. Why did I think I had?"

I shudder.

The woman must have seen me shudder, for she steps closer and rubs my back with the palm of her hand, as if she's trying to chase away my chill.

"You could catch a cold lying on the ground like that," she tells me nicely. "Even on a pleasant day like this."

I heard a thump, turned to look, and saw that the man had dropped the book to the ground. He looked up at me looking down at the book. When I look up at him, he smiles. I can't decide whether I like his smile. No need to make a decision right now, I remind myself.

The woman starts rubbing my back again. Her orange freckles glow like bright paint against her light skin. When I say—not to her but to myself—that her hair is not as strong-white as mine, what I mean is her hair is so meagerly pigmented I think I can say in truth that I can see right through each individual strand of her hair. Her teeth, however, are very white. And the inside of her mouth is quite red. Her smile makes my stomach growl. I wish I had heard what she said to me after those first three words of hers. I expect she thinks I did hear her and that I'm now operating with whatever knowledge I would have gained if I had heard her. But I didn't hear her, and I'll never know what she said.

Crack!

The man kicked the book away from him. Is his problem with the book or with my having commented on it? Beats me. Fourteen. Fourteen. Fourteen. Fourteen. I repeat the magic number to myself. *Fourteen* four times is powerful protection.

I may not need the protection of numbers. I may already have all the protection I need in these two strangers. These people could have appeared out of thin air to be my guardians. And I could have appeared out of thin air to be their ward. And the grass could have appeared out of thin air to be my resting place while I waited for these new protectors to materialize. Yes, everywhere one looks there are myriad possibilities. That is the nature of things. Or so I've heard tell.

What's his name? I don't see it written anywhere on him or on his clothes. He could be nameless. Or his name might be a secret. Even the woman, Zole, maybe doesn't know his name. Until I hear differently, I'll just call him Felix. Zole and Felix.

Oh! There's some words. Felix may have a name of his own after all. A twilight-blue, 3x5 card is working its way up out of his shirt pocket. The words are a fluorescent pinkish-red, bordered in black. "Texture Gels," the card says. That would be an interesting name. Wait! Here comes some more, another line of words. "For Dimensional Effects." Zingo! A five-word name! I could get jealous of that. I don't have even a three-word name. Immediately, I have to come up with a plan to keep myself from getting all worked up. That's easy enough: I'll be a rascal and refuse to call him anything but *Felix*, no matter how he protests.

There goes the card. It slid back down into his

pocket.

I look up at Felix's eyes. He's looking at my eyes. He reaches into his pocket, takes out the card, crumples it into a tight little wad, and tosses it over his shoulder, as if to say, Felix it is. I chalk up another victory for my naming ability.

Hey! It just occurred to me that Felix is a memory of me. How would that work? Whew! I'd have to construct an entirely different way of looking at the world, wouldn't I. I'd have to make a great effort. And how would I explain Zole then? Already I can feel the idea slipping away. We will be three separate people, Zole and Felix and me, three individuals, forever.

Why did I say "forever"? Did this word mysteriously enter my brain from some other level of existence where I know things that I don't know here and now?

Zole stops rubbing my back. "Do you feel OK now?" she asks me. I like her voice, I'm sure of that, even though it's a little too glassy for its own good. I nod my head. I would like to possess some of her freckles, a couple dozen or so. She has plenty she could spare. But I won't ask for them. She will have to volunteer them on her own. Otherwise it would not really be a giving.

+

It's getting dark earlier.

It's dark enough now. Now I lay me down to sleep. I lay me down, but before I sleep I check the white. It's there, same size, same shape, same place on dark ground. No, I've never reached out and touched it. The first time I noticed it—that would be the first night I slept here—my first instinct was to look up to see where the light was coming from. But I did not look up. I told myself—and to this day I still see it that way—that the white was a maker of its own light, that it was a small white-light-making area on the ground.

Once I thought I saw something in the light. Next morning, however, I was sure it had been a dream.

-2-

DO UP

Up. Up and at 'em. Up and rat 'em. Sup and bat
'em. The white is gone. The day is almost upon us. In what
body am I waking up this morning?

I get up from the ground and run around a big
circle, round and round, slapping my hands against the sides
of my thighs and slapping them together above my head,
over and over. Repetitions! Repetitions! I then switch to a
triangle and run the three sides of its perimeter. This
morning's triangle fits inside of this morning's circle with its
three angle points just touching the circle. Next I do a
square, then an ellipse that gradually flattens to a line. The
line loses its two-directionality and becomes the route out
of here.

I stop my energetic trotting quite a ways before I get
to the tree, not wanting to be so noticeable that someone
would be watching me when I climb up into the tree. Wait!
I stop and hunker down close to the ground. There's a big
yellow truck parked at the curb, and three men—city
maintenance personnel?—are looking up into the tree. Are
they looking for me? No…I don't think so. Woe is me! One
of them went back to the truck and is now walking toward
my tree with a powersaw. I can't look. What to do? Don't
panic! Just in the nick of time I remember a fitting section
of a conversation I had recently unintentionally/unwillingly
overheard, a conversation between two oldsters of mixed
gender about the undesirability of thoughts of revenge.
"Change your routine instead, mister. Find something else

to do first thing in the morning." I say a crisp goodbye to Hossmattcha-in-the-sky and head out to unknown parts of this part of the main part of the universe.

"Main part of the universe" sounds a bit egotistical, doesn't it, even if I didn't mean it that way. Zip! Just like that, I'm warping the truth again to sound righteous. How could I mean it, "main part of the universe," any other way? I would think that a person can be not-elitist from time to time, but is it truly possible for anyone to ever be not-self-centered? My answer at the moment would be a resounding no. When a local glee club then pops up above the buildings to sing boomingly to me a stinging scolding, "You're wrong, you're wrong, you're wrong," what can I do but smile?

I'm still making my way away from the tree and into another life when my mind suddenly becomes heavy. One's head can become heavy, one's thoughts can become heavy, but one's mind? Well…that's what it feels like, my mind has gotten heavy. Then, quick, a subtle shadow descends out of thin ether to become the delicate, flexing surface of my mind.

As if that isn't enough to upset this person, me, before breakfast, I now see coming over the horizon a huge self-propelled machine. It's black and grey with thin vertical stripes of deep red and dark blue. Should I recognize this shapeless contraption, or is it something new to me? It's got a long arm reaching up into the sky, on the end of which is a mechanical hand. Dangling from that hand is a torn white shirt. In the folds of the shirt is the word *Help*. The machine rumbles on by me. I spin about to watch it disappear. Or was that word *Hello*? The day is upon us.

"Usually, what is fine comes after what is rough."

The tone of the exceptionally short person standing at attention before me was so aggressive that her or his statement sounded more like a challenge to a fistfight than anything else. I swear she/he is so severely rumpled that she/he looks like an overworked and then discarded paper towel. No question mark was there to be heard at the end of the sentence aimed right at me from this person's vocal cords; even so, I say back as if I were answering a question, "Yes, I think I would agree. Usually. If you're looking at the world from that certain direction, then that is *usually* true. But if you look from another direction, the opposite order—rough coming after fine—might just as easily be seen as the norm."

I'm certain you're already tired of me separating two personal pronouns by a little rod (/)—see the wonky paragraph above. Therefore, either I will have to come up with a name for this person or I will have to not mention this person again. Making the decision whether to name or to forget is not easy for me, on this occasion. I think I will turn my back to this person momentarily to see if that makes deciding any easier for me.

I turn away, and the world all of a sudden becomes totally quiet. This is wonderful. If the world were forever quiet…

Curiosity. Is curiosity stronger than pleasure? I can't say if curiosity is *always* the stronger, but it is this time. I turn back around.

The world is *not* quiet, and the person before me is

no longer "exceptionally short" or of indefinite gender. *She* is as tall as me and startlingly beautiful—smooth, perfectly smooth, not a wrinkle anywhere, the kind of beauty you are afraid to touch. Her name is Taxi. I turn away again.

I turn away and the world is immaculately quiet.

I turn back around to face the woman, not knowing what to expect. I find that the world is again full of noise and that she, Taxi, has aged drastically. Wrinkles and discoloration, everywhere.

She repeats her sentence. "Usually, what is fine comes after what is rough."

I bow my head in understanding.

That would be nice if that were true; it isn't; I don't understand anything! I examine her sentence from one end and then from the other end. I see the way she looks now and remember how she looked just a few moments ago. Up is up and down is down, but up is also down and down is also up. I call her by name, "Taxi."

She looks way down into my eyes (probably ignoring the backs of my eyeballs) and smiles slyly. "Thank you. I like that name. I've been given names before, but I like that one. *Taxi*."

+

"Who is this *we?*"

No, I don't think we have reached the point yet where we can discuss our personal identities, if, indeed, we have personal identities. Just tag along please.

That's an interesting word, *identities*. It looks like a little mountain range.

Taxi is gone. She was cremated last week. We walked together to the building where she was to be burned up. She told me as we went in the last door she would ever step through that the service would be brief and that she belonged to no clubs or organizations of any kind. "So," she said proudly, "you will be able to set through it with no sweat." I didn't recognize the saying "no sweat." Someone kindly explained it to me later. She was right, though. I didn't go to sleep, I didn't have to leave before I threw up, I didn't jump to my feet and shout, "That's crap! That there is an insult!"

I just sat there like an uprooted treetrunk and cried. The tears were a surprise. I didn't know what they meant. But crying in a big room with other people paying you no mind at all was refreshing.

Taxi died at twenty-five. I don't know if that is young to die or old. I hadn't known her long, yet I was confident she had led a full life, as the speaker at the service said she had. Up! Up from the ground she rose, like a wisp of smoke above a snuffed candle.

Wouldn't you just know it? I'm thinking now about smokestacks. Here comes another memory associated with Taxi, probably the last one: As I stepped out into the fresh air, I saw *smokestacks* spelled SMKSTKS on a license plate on a shiny car parked alongside the burn-em-up building.

+

Listen to this, please. "I do, of course, easily be converted to out-of-house thinking." Now tell me if you will, did that sound to you like an uneducated sentence, a sentence said in jest, or a profound explanation of a problem that the speaker has had all their livelong life but didn't know about until this very minute? I'm asking because...

"Hi."

"Hello there. Fancy seeing you again. I was just thinking about you."

"Because you saw me coming?"

"I did not see you coming. You took me by surprise. I was mulling over something you said yesterday?"

"The only thing I said to you yesterday as we passed each other on the sidewalk for the first time ever was my patent *hi*, just like the one I gave you here on the same piece of sidewalk today."

"That's not quite true. I distinctly heard you say to my back, 'I do, of course, easily be converted to out-of-house thinking.' And don't deny it." He is a tall, skinny man. Handsome, wily, probably not to be trusted. But he is definitely interesting to look at. And his voice has so much character that he seems to be talking on five different levels at the same time. I will let him tell me his name himself.

"Mack."

"Mack?" My naming ability would never have reached the *m*'s for this guy.

"Right. Do you like it?"

"I've never known anyone named Mack. It has a big, broad, jutting sound to it."

"Most people say that *Mack* fits me just perfectly." He shrugs his thin shoulders, then raises his head.

"You mean it fits your personality perfectly, don't you?"

"That's what I said."

"Mack what?"

"Mack March."

"You have a two-word name?"

"Two is enough for me. How many have you got?"

"Two too. Why did you say that to me yesterday?"

"The hi or the sentence you said I said."

"Are you saying now that you did not say it?"

"Oh, I said it all right." Mack turns away from me. He turns his back to me and forms a tall *little t* by extending both his arms straight out to his sides. Then he turns to stone.

I walk around in front of him. Mack winks at me. He doesn't lower his arms, though. Or say anything.

+

If you want to know if I am going to tell Mack March my name, the quickest answer I know is no. Not today anyway. If I told him my name, then you would know it, too. And I'm still not ready for all that.

+

I get it! I get it! I get it! Mack has his back to me with his arms out because that is how he was standing when he said to me, "I do, of course, easily be converted to out-of-house thinking." And that means I'm supposed to turn my back to him as if we are walking away from each other like we were yesterday.

Quickly I return to his backside. Stopping a couple

of steps behind him, I turn my back to him and reach one of my arms out in front of me and stick my other arm out behind me, as if I am striding away. Eyes ahead.

"So I sort of recall that the sun is shining here in the usually foggy belt."

I stop myself before quipping that it is never foggy here. Is this an example of his "out-of-house thinking"? What do I do now? Walk on away, as I did yesterday; and tomorrow we will meet here again and do this all over again? I cannot hear his steps behind me. I turn just my head and look. He has turned his head and is gazing at me.

How long can we stand like this? It's like a stare-down contest. I don't know that I want to do this till I drop. But I could, I guess. No, why should I.

As I turn to face him, he turns to face me. My arms are still sticking out ahead and behind me. He reaches out his hand and takes my front hand. He grips me firmly and doesn't let go. Do I have a problem?

"I am glad to meet you," he says in a deeper yet still multi-leveled voice. "I understand that you don't want to tell me your name."

My mouth drops open. He's so straight-out-with-it.

"So," he continues, "I will give you a name that I can call you by. And if you ever want to use this name other than with me, it's OK. It's quite all right."

He steps toward me so that he can press my hand against his chest. I let my back hand drop to my side. He lowers his chin devoutly. He has not shaved today.

"My name for you is Ial."

"Isle, like a small island?"

"No. I-a-l. It sort of sounds like *isle*, but it is not

quite the same."

"Ial?"

"That's it. That's exactly how it's said. Ial."

Am I now a suffix? His suffix?

+

The light! The patch of white has followed me to
this new place to sleep. I'm asleep. No! I'm not. There is
something forming on the light on the ground—a woman, a
white woman with crystal hair. Her two hands are full of
bits of orange peel. Correction—the bits are not orange
peel, they are freckles. The woman is offering them to me.

+

Ial is only for the Mack-to-me-to-Mack connection.
I have no intention to replace my real name. I get up from
the ground in my usual fashion but don't run around any
geometric figures this morning. Where is this place that I
find myself in?

I look around but don't recognize anything. I could
be anywhere. Hardly! See the color of the sky behind those
buildings? This is the same big booming burg I have woken
up in every morning since the beginning of the world. In
fact, if I squint my eyes just right and glimpse way down
between this and that, I can just make out the chocolate
spot on the sidewalk where Mack and I had our now
famous passing the day before yesterday and our more
famous naming session yesterday.

Should I go down to stand on that spot and wait for

him? I might have to stand there for eighteen months or more. Or he might already be there waiting for me by the time I get down there. Tis the first unanswerable question of the morning. When things get tough, what do I always do? Wrong. I never hide. Almost never. I wait for a news release from wisdom.

I expect that sounded ho-key. I said "wisdom" because, wherever these messages come from, there has to be a lot of wiseness there. The messages are always dead-on.

The real problem is getting these messages to come to me. Usually I just climb up into a tree and wait. Or if there's no tree willing to have me, I sit on a protuberance of a building and wait. It often seems that my sitting posture makes a difference in how long it is before I get a hit. That may not be true, though. It's possible that I might just be more comfortable waiting in a certain posture.

Is there any place like that around here for me to sit? Hey! There's a chair parked over there alongside that building. It's a rickety-looking old metal contraption, but it just might hold me up long enough for a word from wisdom to get here.

I walk directly over to the chair, position the chair to my liking, and gingerly lower my butt down on it. I no more than get myself carefully sat down when Mack March comes walking along the side of the building. See! Sitting on the chair was a good posture.

He stops beside me to stare down at me. We exchange smiles. The young sun is on us, warming us. From where I am sitting Mack looks as tall as the building. I can see the faces of children in his hair. There are monkey faces in there, too. And that's a zebra head…a dog with a long tongue…a bluebangled bomber…a charley horse.

"There had better be at least one muffin left!"

I grin up nervously at him, not knowing what to make of his threatening statement.

A bag of something! I hadn't noticed that Mack had kept one hand behind his back all this time. He held this bag out until I took it from him.

What would I guess is in the bag? Mack mentioned muffins; so it might be muffins. Or if not muffins, then some other kind of food. The bag's about the right weight to contain food. Or there could be plants in the bag, plants that he dug up to present to me—a little dirt, roots, stems and leaves. Maybe some flowers too. Food and plants are both from nature. What if the bag holds something unnatural? Like what? Plastic toys…see-thru shoes…bright yellow tools, to offer three examples off the top of my head.

Mack slowly rolls his body to lean his forehead against the building. "Open it, please," he says plaintively.

That smacks of a good method of proceeding. Yet I hesitate to open the bag. Death, injury, damage? What if this is a bag of poisonous reptiles? Oh, well, life has been a sweet pumping up of the mind to no avail.

"It's muffins!" honk I.

"Didn't I give you a big clue, Ial." Mack is still pressing his forehead against the rough wall. I hope he doesn't poke a hole in his skin.

"Sure you did. But…"

"Sure I did, but—"

How about a short list of funny words to distract from my present uncomfortableness? *Gibe. Cronyism. Polar bear. Hosepipe. Cissoid.* Five is sufficient, I should think.

The words are not particularly funny? Good, that's even better. You can use my unhumorous words of choice as *revealing*. In other words, those five words will allow you to see what kind of uncomfortable I am.

They don't? The words are not particularly revealing? I really don't understand that. I always thought that everything is revealing. Even *a complete coverup* reveals a need to hide something.

And speaking of coverups, I will now pull a cover up.

+

Two. Naked people. Two naked people lying on the grass in their backyard. Two naked people sitting up to sip at their glasses of pale liquid. They don't say anything to each other. I've been told that naked people have nothing to say. They lie back down. I wonder at the depressions they are making in the grass. One of them sits back up, sees me, waves a big friendly wave.

+

Two clothed people. Two people clothed in uniforms, jet black uniforms with lots of tinsel, lots of silvery patches and stripes and cantilevered ledges cryptically arranged on midnight warcloth and leather. Enraptured by their own meretricious brightness-on-darkness, the pair, a man and a woman with ravaged faces, strut toward me, arrogantly examining every move that I make, as if it is me and not them who is dressed like them. Each of the two is wearing a long-barreled gun. Everything close to the guns is black (no silver allowed there), as are the guns themselves, so that, I assume, the "shooting irons" are not so obvious. "They're packing heat!" That punchy warning I picked off a theater poster. Not to be the contrary sort, but I thought the poster should have said, "They're packing *de-heat-ers!*"

+

Two naked people? Two clothed people? What am I talking about? What am I thinking about? (More often than not, the two, talking and thinking, are heading in divergent directions in and about my head.) No, I'm not thinking about guns, not anymore.

+

I am the green deity up on the grassy knoll overlooking the bird pens. A giant raven in a round cage that looks as if it were designed to hold a tiger is staring back at the green avatar. The green avatar stares back at the black raven, calls him an overweight common crow, asks him how many little fingers of little girls he has bitten off today. The raven calls back haughtily, daring the deity to come closer. The deity thumbs the avatar's nose at the raven. The raven stamps hotly about his pen, flapping his big strong wings, screaming his most obscene sounds. I just met the bird today, but it looks like a lasting friendship could develop between us.

Should I throw back the cover? OK.

"Hi." Mack March sits down beside me. "Do you

enjoy picking on caged birds, Ial?"

"He's my new friend," softly although confidently I answer. "We are developing a common language, complete with gestures, escapes, blocks, afflictive emotions, common grounds, subtle and coarse sayings, subtle and coarse blisses, subtle and coarse insights."

"Are you and I going to develop a common language?"

"No, I don't think so, Mack. Unless we make some kind of *miraculous* breakthrough, I think that you and I are stuck with ice-cube-sized islands of language in the huge warm ocean of language."

Mack rolls his eyes up. "The singer whispered, 'Marietto.'"

Mack must be looking at the sky. Surely he can't see the scrawny tree behind us. "Right, Mack. Exactly. That was a perfect example of one ice-cube-sized island of language, a product, I suspect, of your *out-of-house thinking.*"

"Gotcha!" Mack's eyes drop to the tip of my nose. "I couldn't make out at first what you were talking about. But I understand now, I think." Mack then shakes his head over-seriously. "That's me. But what about you? You don't talk like that."

"But I do. I haven't around you yet, M&M, yet I most certainly have my own brand of out-of-house thinking and speaking."

With this admission, the cover drops again.

+

Now where were we before Mack showed up? And

before I got to talking to the bird? "Two naked people…two clothed people…what am I talking about…"? Yes, that is what we were discussing. And it looks like I now have something further to say. Clearly I was at fault in presenting such contrasting pictures of those four people—the two amiable nakeds on the grass and, following close on their tails, the intimidating two fully attired in silver and black. I probably don't do that, oversimplification of complex social problems, any more than anyone else; but I do do it often.

"So what's the problem?"

Did I just hear a cliché used unrhetorically? You want to know what exactly are the problems I was referring to when I so facilely spat out, "…oversimplification of complex social problems…"? The problems that come to mind are the great, people-splitting gaps between the five tastes. (Hah! Surprised you, didn't I. You expected me to comeback with something like, "It was a joke, silly person." You didn't think I would be able to construct anything that could be used as an answer before tomorrow sometime.) Sweet, sour, bitter, astringent, pungent. That may not be the same list of fundamental tastes that you prefer to use. You may use the list that has salty in it. Added salt is not a basic in my diet, and the taste of salt is to me a composite of tastes. So I use a different list of basic tastes. I found that the nakeds taste sweet and slightly astringent, while the intimidating two taste sour and bitter and a touch pungent. One can get so used to a taste or a combo of tastes that other tastes or combos are not tolerated. Clearly I am at fault. I should not have been so hidebound as to pretend that I still remember the rules-that-divide, rules so old and arbitrary that I can no longer recall where I first heard them or under what conditions they might have worked OK at one time or whether I have in fact *never* heard them and am just making all this up.

+

Decarie. Would that be a first or a last name? I prefer to use it as a first name, though it's probably used mostly as a last.

The news this morning: "Cutthroats attack village!"

The news this noon: "Thousands flee flooding river!"

I wonder if the two events are related. They could be, you know. There are many ways that these two occurrences could be tied together. Yeah, such is the stuff of the entertainment industry. Or is that trade still called *show business?*

If I were composing the lead news article for this afternoon, what would I write about? Nothing absolutely banal like cutthroating and thousands fleeing, you can be sure. Hmm. My title would read: "The World Is Not Living Up To My Expectations!" Whew! Did I sound like a spoiled, eight year old brat? But isn't that title of mine true for most adults? Who out there everywhere is getting what they expected to get? I'm not talking about money or power or position. If you were a drawing, what I'm talking about would be the line under your feet, the line that represents the floor or the ground you are standing on.

That didn't make any sense. What was I trying to say? I think I need to lie down now.

3

DECARIE

"Decarie is the name."

Decarie is a doll. *Doll* as in "a small-scale figure of a human being." Not *doll* as in "a young, baby-faced featherbrain, usually female." I sit up, rub the sleep from my eyes, and ask, "First or last?" The small man sits down on the ground facing me with his legs out in front of him. His shoes are not any larger than I would have expected them to be.

"Which first-or-last?" he asks in a jovial voice, though he is not smiling. Nor is he frowning. He just looks real and is talking as if he is thoroughly enjoying the moment, as if he is the perfect presence.

"First or last name."

"First. It's my first name."

I nod my head in approval. "Good. That's the way I saw it yesterday." The man doesn't look small—he just isn't the size one would expect someone who looks like he does to be.

"You saw Decarie as my first name yesterday?"

"No, I had no assurance yesterday that anyone named Decarie actually exists. I saw your name as *a*—that *a* was stressed for emphasis and will be repeated for the same reason—*a* first name yesterday."

Decarie crosses his legs out in front of him and leans back on his arms, spreading the fingers of his hands on the ground behind him. "And what if I said back to you, 'Good, that's the way I saw it yesterday, too.'"

"I would then be totally confused, Decarie, as confused as I already am by just the possibility of your saying what you just said."

"Excellent. Now we are both confused. That puts us on more even ground."

"That is important to you?"

"It is."

So I cross my legs out in front of me and spread my hands behind me. "We are now equal?"

"Equality is not what I need. It's equal opportunity. If given a fair starting point, I always win."

He said that. He did. I am at a loss as to what I should return with.

That real face grins. I can see why Decarie doesn't normally grin, if he doesn't. He says from between his drawn-back lips, "I shocked you."

I admit it. "You certainly did."

"Then we are now on even more even ground, because your being here this morning shocked *me*."

"Is this your place, Decarie?"

"No," he sunnily replies—the disconcerting grin had vanished immediately after he told me he had shocked me. "My place is over there. This is no one's place. The fact that somebody was lying here is what gave me a jolt."

"You want your ideas viewed in the best possible light. Right?"

Decarie's head jerks from side to side several times. Then he does that grin again. Understanding has come to him. "I don't know what that meant, why you said something like that; but I think I know where it came from. *You* are the person who was seen with Mack March yesterday. Am I right? Mack spins off like that when he's talking with people, too."

"You know Mack March, Decarie?"

"Doesn't everyone?"

"I guess so." I try to copy his grin, can't do it. "At least everyone here with us so far this morning."

"Did you have sex?"

"Who? Mack and me?"

"Yes."

"No."

"Oh." Decarie looks disappointed, though he is no less cheerful.

I wink at him and uncross my legs to raise my knees and bring my feet together close to me.

Decarie lowers his eyes. "I won't ask you any more personal questions like that."

And I tell him the truth. "Thank you. I would appreciate that."

"Did he give you a name?"

"Yes, Decarie, he did." I ask myself, does Mack March name everyone? "Ial."

"Ial... That sounds like a Mack name all right." Decarie starts rolling his head and neck in a circle, and while his mouth is going round and round, he asks, "Mind if I call you that, too?"

I nearly yell at him to stop rolling his head; it's making me woozy. But he stops the circling by himself. His presence has become a little less than perfect. "I don't mind, Decarie."

Then, in a serious tone, I add, "No, and Mack shouldn't mind either. He told me point-blank that it's all right for me to use the name other than with him."

What have I gotten myself into here? I see myself watching someone straightening their golden socks. I see myself standing before someone, someone else, watching as their smooth beauty decays and dies before my eyes. Just memories of times past, I remind myself. There's no need to repeat the title: "The World Is Not Living Up To My Expectations!"

That sounded a bit like the onset of depression, didn't it? NEVER YIELD TO DEPRESSION!

My puny warning goes unheeded. It's a moonless night. A dark vessel sails into view and pulls alongside the wharf. A ramp is lowered and two darkly draped persons come down to get me. They escort me onto the ghostship and drop me into the black hold.

+

I awaken in a dazzling world of white. Drums are playing softly in the distance. The air smells of…what? I think it's a medicinal smell from the day I was born.

The drums might be only the blood pulsing in my head. I think there is someone beside me. It's a woman. She's looking down at me. Ivory skin, pale hair, no orange freckles. Blue eyes.

There's someone to the other side of me. A man. Dark hair, medium dark skin. Scars on his neck.

I can't think of anything to say in the da-da-dazzling white. Then I remember that old one: "Take me to your leader."

+

I awake not to a committee of judges but to clothes bedabbled with blood. Whose blood? Whose clothes?

No blood. No clothes. It's only a dream, sweetheart.

A bloody dream. A first for me.

There is no one beside me, on either side or top or bottom of me.

Am I lying on my back on the ground? Yes. I spread my fingers on the dirt. I raise my feet and drop them to the dirt. I lift my head and drop it to the dirt.

"Have a heart." I see those words on a sign that's floating high in the blue sky above me. The sign is meant for me, I know it. I throw my hands to my chest to see if I do have a heart, if I ever had a heart. Yes, I can feel it thumping in there. So, what is new?

Should I sit up to see where I am? What if I don't recognize where I am? That's an easy one: I could then just lie back down on the dirt. Wait! There is something scribbled on my heart. "Alice Loves Ya."

Who is this Alice and why does she think she can write on me?

Maybe this Alice is not a person. Maybe *Alice* stands for some grand idea, some wondrous concept.

I wonder if *Alice & Bill* is a doubly complex concept. Maybe Bill left a note somewhere on my backside. Would the note read "Bill Loves Ya, Too"? Or would it clue me in that Bill has despised me forever?

Maybe Bill is a club, an elitist group with plans to write hateful reminders on the butts of everyone who sleeps on the ground. That sounds like a good guess.

Sit up! And I do it.

And what do I see? I see you.

+

The part he is pointing at could conceivably read just as he said, "…both superficial and systematic disorders…." But what I see printed there is "…gloss medium and varnish together…." I tell him that, and he says back to me with a shrug of his shoulders, "Same thing."

I back away from the sign on the pole. Mack told me that the sign is advertising a lecture to be given any day now by an eminent scholar, whom I have never heard of. But I think Mack's wrong. I think the sign is nothing more than a how-to-do-it teaser from a plastic paint company. Mack carefully frees the paper from the pole and folds it up and stuffs it into his pocket. I wonder why he wants that in his pocket.

Then he verbalizes a bit of his out-of-house thinking. For me? "Most people spell the word b-r-a-k-e-s in this situation. Let me know, please, if I am in error on this matter."

I can't resist stuttering (stuttering is a friend of mine), "I love t-t-tomatoes almost as much as I love p-p-potatoes."

Mack smiles broadly. He is smiling not off to one side but directly at me. I think he's very pleased with me. He says, to me, in a regal voice, "Walking thru walls. Not to mention. Walking thru walls into consequences."

If I were to say something right now, something like, "If successful…," I think Mack would fill in the blank instantly, the very instant that he realized it was a blank, as if he had no need to bother thinking first. I can't guess what his reply would be, probably something succinct like "…then proceed." And I'm sure he would come right back with a blank of his own for me to fill in. "If too thin…," he might say. I myself would have to think first, even if it appeared that I was answering very quickly. "…add more mass, but avoid getting yourself a thick, buttery body." Mack would probably laugh at the thought of a buttery body. He's so thin himself. The very first things I noticed about him—not the first time I saw him but the first time that I talked to him—is that he is tall, he is skinny, he is good-looking, and in a certain indescribable way he is definitely not to be trusted. I repeat my question to myself, What have I gotten myself into here? Where do I go from here? I've started feeling foul around Mack.

+

It was Decarie who turned me off to Mack. "…turned me off to…"? I don't know if that's a natural way to say what I'm trying to say or not. I'm thinking right now that it may be a misleading construction. So I'll restate my declaration, clear and simple: It was a result of my meeting Decarie that I lost interest in Mack. Or was that sentence structure confusing too?

When I close my eyes, I see Decarie's grin. I'm also fairly certain that Decarie too got his name from Mack. At least D. didn't have to suffer a suffix for a tag.

Enough of this. A few salty oaths. Saving me the ignominy. The geographic center of…

+

The geographic center of this tree is me. Me in a tree. A new tree. In a grove of trees with mowed grass.

A most wonderful junction of limbs fits my body perfectly. Four limbs form the most elegant chaise lounge I've ever encountered or even seen. I can lie on my back, on either side, or even on my stomach if I'm so inclined.

Don't get me wrong now: it's not a jungle that I'm putting up in. In spite of the many trees, the area is open and quite bright and airy. Do you remember that I mentioned mowed grass? There are flowers too. Some of the trees, not mine, have little curved pieces of concrete lined up in a circle around where the trunk goes into the ground. Everything hereabouts is nice and proper.

Except me, of course. The nicest thing about me is you. And the most proper thing about me is...

I couldn't finish that last sentence. No, I didn't have an emotional problem. I just couldn't decide what was most proper about me. No, that's not true. It's not that I couldn't *decide*; I would have to have at least two things to decide between before I could do any deciding.

Now if I were oared, I just might row this tree way up higher in the sky. Singing all the while I would be. Singing about being in the sky, singing about being in love with the sky, singing about being not quite alive, singing about being a being with hands and teeth and one roundish bellybutton. I am not a young shoot, I am not a well-developed tree. I am not oared.

Now if I were bored instead of oared, I just might

wonder where the blinking dapples on the wood go. They might just disappear from here to then immediately reappear somewhere else on the branch or even on me, but I doubt that. No, the dapples dance over the edge of the branch to go where? "Into the past," seems a non-answer. "Into the depths of the present," seems a tad more workable as an answer. However! If we get rid of the past, don't we have to do likewise with the present? And what place do I (or anyone else, I assume) occupy in all of this? Hear the shout from afar, "I am the absolute perceiver!" Whence then did come all your troubles, I rejoin. Another shout blasts from the opposite direction, "Get rid of your *I*, my friend, and then you will *see*." Harrumph! That must have been a joke. How can I be rid of my *I*, I want to know. A third strong voice calmly offers a solution. "How does a rock get rid of its *rock*? It puts its *rock* in the middle of a stream of water and keeps it there until there is no more rock." That sounds reasonable, I say sarcastically; all I need then is the patience of stone. "Patience is easy," says that third voice. "For patience is only a lack of choice." My one and only and very puny reply to that is that there is never a complete lack of choice. Quickly I separate myself from the voices. How? I just stopped listening to them. Are they the voices I use to talk with myself? That would be convenient if they were, but that doesn't seem to be the case. They sounded so much like the voices of people passing below, people saying things that fit well into what I was thinking about. True, oppression can *convince* me that there are no choices and freedom (insight) can *show* me that there are no choices. Demonstrate—

I look down and see a cat climbing up. Is this his

(I'll relate to the cat as a male, for no special reason, until I learn otherwise) tree? Here I thought it was my tree. But it might well be his.

Cat climbs up to me and onto me. He puts his front paws on my chest and stretches his body to stare into my eyes. He says, "Meow." I say, "Meow." We both say at the same time, "Meo-o-ow." He promptly lies down and goes to sleep on me. I lean my head back against the tree's thickest branch and go to sleep, too.

+

The sun is up. The sun is down. The sun is up. The sun is up. Up is the sun. Up am I. Up in our tree am I. Cat's gone out for a walk. Maybe he'll bring back some breakfast for us.

Someone is under the tree looking up at me. A very agreeable-to-look-at woman. Clear-cut features on a delicate skull. Tan skin. Thick, dark, wavy hair. Flowing, finely-woven cloth. High, black, snap-to-close boots. She has reached her hand up at me.

She's holding up little pink things to me! What in this wide woolly world could they be? There's no way she's going to climb up into this tree with those clothes on; so, assuming she is not going to take the clothes off, I guess I am going to have to climb down to her. Which I, of course, do. In high spirits.

"I am Madeleine. Madeleine Phitt," she says to me in an effortless, pleasingly present voice. And when she sees that I am smiling at her but am not going to give her my name in return, she says, "I have brought you these." She offers to put the pink things in my hand, which I have reflexively raised.

She notices the quizzical look on my face and grins big for me. She has marvelous teeth. "They are throbs." She drops them onto my hand.

My eyes bulge a bit as I try to hook up the word *throb* with what I see on my hand. If they look like anything, they look like five big pink pills.

Madeleine perceives my predicament and instructs me. "Put one of them in your mouth and you will understand why they are called throbs."

Does she truly think that I am going to take something offered by a complete stranger and put it in my mouth? Yes, the beautiful stranger does think that.

It tastes vaguely like cinnamon, slides easily down my throat. And then I understand why its called a throb. My entire body throbs, gently. It's a most agreeable sensation. My body throbs like that eleven times while a warm glow is settling over me. I look around for my voice to ask, "What was that?"

"Food."

I call her by the name she has given herself. "Really, Madeleine? Food?"

"A new food. Highly concentrated."

"What prompted you to bring me food?"

"My cat led me here a half of an hour ago. It looked as if you hadn't eaten yet today, if not for some longer period. I went home and got those. Is that answer enough?"

"And where is your cat now, Madeleine?"

"Above you."

It's true. The one and the same Cat was lying right

where I had been lying up in the tree. He *had* brought me food.

I won't even think of saying that Phitt is a Phitting name.

+

"Do I take all of them right now?"

"No, it is not a good idea to take more than one at a time. Five is a day's worth."

"Where does one get these things, Madeleine?"

I swear the way she looked at me made me want to chew on her lip in the dark. Just looking at her lower lip, right now, makes my body feel like a needle, not that same "needle in a haystack" but a lone sewing needle falling as if forever from the top of a tall building.

"They are readily available. Most food stores stock them." We have started walking. We are not heading anywhere; we are just meandering. Cat chose to not come with us. Madeleine continues, "After you have ingested maybe ten days worth, you don't notice the throbs anymore. They go away. Your body has gotten used to the new food. Yet the name *throbs* has stuck. Everyone calls them that." She takes my hand as we stroll along. I feel the heat inside her body.

I know she is shucking me. I know the pinkies are a drug of some kind. But I don't rightly care. I am suffering no ill effects. In fact the only effect I do notice (make out) is a slight heightening of my sexual interest, not sexual interest in Madeleine, just sexual interest in general. Holding hands with another person is feeling so good. So, maybe the pinkies are an aphrodisiac. Hmm. Let's hope they are organic anyway.

Tiger. Tiger. Tiger. Tiger. Where is the tiger?

Why am I repeating the word *tiger*? Is Madeleine a tiger? That would be interesting. What is a tiger other than a nine-to-twelve-foot-long striped cat? I will dial up some definitions. "Fierce and blood thirsty." Perhaps that Phitts, but I think probably not. "A vigorously aggressive person, usually highly skilled at something." That sounds more like the aspect whose name I was repeating. It follows then that I should now be curious. What is Madeleine hyper aggressive about and what is she so very skilled at?

Stop! I stop myself from further constructing an idle fantasy about a person whose only abnormalities may be her wearing of fine clothes, her need to feed strangers, and her great hand-holding ability. But! I think of *tiger* again.

I didn't mention it before: there was what looked to be a word on the pinkie I swallowed, but the letters were either truncated or too small to read. Or if they weren't letters at all, maybe they were a drawing. Or a map, a map to the source of the pinkies, to their creator. There are four leftover pinkies, which I put in my pocket. To get one out to examine it, I would have to let go of Madeleine, which I do not want to do.

I look up the definitions of words fairly frequently, don't I? Where do I look them up? I don't know. Did I sit down one month and memorize a dictionary? A BIG dictionary, rich in content, with a great information structure that, unfortunately, is often cryptic to new visitors, but with clear guidelines and overwhelmingly GOOD NEWS, as well as millions of insights and numerous peeks behind the scenes with special focus on becoming a master of repetitive tasks, making it incumbent on me to teach. Who knows! Could be! Should I ask Madeleine? No, I'd say that that is generally not a good idea at this time. Because if she does know, while I don't know, wouldn't that be something else? We'd have to stop right here and stare into each other's eyes. It would get darker and darker until we could no longer see each other's eyes, but we would keep on staring until Cat comes to rescue us.

"Sure, I recognized you the moment I saw you up in that tree," says Madeleine, her words winding out of her mouth like a gentle sea breeze. Watching her words blow away from me, I realize that just because she was a stranger to me, that didn't necessarily make me a stranger to her. I think of blackish green spit. Who is this Madeleine and what does she want from me? She squeezes my hand to keep me from letting go of hers.

Guess what the next thing that she said to me was. "If you don't help me, I will surely die." Yep, she told me that she recognized me and then she said that I would have to help her or she would die. Nice package. Which way do I run?

+

Which way indeed!

I skyrocket straight up in the air, not slowing my headlong levitation one bit before I am upwards of two miles high in the sky. Then I turn off my rocket to glide silently up and on up and up. I need no oars! Reaching the top, I pause, not to look around, to think, to think thoughts

I have never before thought, assuming it is possible to think a *completely new* thought. Wait! Having a completely new thought is probably *not* possible. Not. It only stands to reason that all those millions of little particles that make up one thought are constantly rearranged and reused, over and over. Anyway, one of my thoughts has to do with "being known." To be or not to be known? Is that a choice that some people of good background get to consciously make? What is the nature of being known? What is the cost? What is the nature of not being known? What is its cost? Is there any difference between being known and not?

I must have been sinking while I was thinking, for I am now gazing down on nine ravens yak-yaking in a tree. I can't actually hear them yet, but I see their beaks opening and closing. Is one of the ravens the one I recently had a conversation with? Has he escaped his cage? I do hope so.

I might not ever know if he has or not, however; for a wind comes up and blows me south. Pressing my hands firmly together above my head and pointing my toes downward, I am a needle again, that lone sewing needle. I drop immediately to the earth.

I land on grass beside a cloth spread over the grass. Stretched out on the cloth is a minimally clothed woman lying in the sun. Her hands are out, away from her body with their palms turned up to the sun. A large straw hat covers her face and hair, to block the sun I assume. Should I introduce myself? Maybe she is asleep under that hat; and if I said anything, I would be a bother. Peering again at one of the woman's hands, I remember how good it felt to hold hands with Madeleine. I stand up and glance around for the tree with the nine birds in it. Nope, I don't see it. So I walk away from the woman before she uncovers her face and gets frightened by my proximity.

4

A WOMAN WITH A HAT COVERING HER FACE

A woman with a hat covering her face. That was yesterday, but I still can't help wondering if I knew her. Why did I just walk away from her? What else could I have done besides walk away? I couldn't very well break into her party just to find out if I'm already there. And that brings up the question of why do some events—my nearly dropping physically onto the hatted woman, for example—stick close to the top and keep spurting up into my attention, while other, equally fascinating experiences—like my shooting up into the sky to escape Madeleine and her pinkies, which I threw out of my pocket on my way way up and away— quickly fade away, unless they are dragged up out of their ghostliness to use as an example in the description of a question I won't try to answer. Cat, raven. Raven, cat. A woman under an alias... A woman masquerading under an indeterminate number of hats... Hey! Do you know what I forgot? I forgot to describe the very cloth she was lying on. Do I remember what the cloth looks like, I ask myself. Did I even notice? Yes, I do/did! It was terry cloth. It was a plain white terry cloth towel. And it had a silver label on one corner. The label said, in red letters, MAIDEN'S WORK. What is a *maiden*, you ask. I don't know for sure, but I think it is a horse of some kind. Yes, I remember now. It is a horse who has never won a race. If a horse wants to win a race so that he or she will no longer be called a maiden, that race will have to be human-sponsored, I'm sure. Horse races only witnessed by other horses don't count. I knew a horse once, by the name of Blinking Bebbs, who had no tail, very little mane, favored her left rear leg, and jumped off a fourteen story cliff in her second year. I never could figure out the suicide note she had delivered to me, posthumously, by her bridlemaker. I shutter and stutter, Was my r-r-remembering B-b-blinking B-b-bebbs a preparation for what is coming n-n-next? (Hah! I'm so inane sometimes.) Well, next, I will say that it is time to consider opening my eyes. It does look like daytime on the other side of my eyelids. Blink! I open my eyes. Blue sky. Tree branches. A tiny yellow-green leaf floating in the air just above my face.

The leaf lands on my nose, and I'm looking cross-eyed at the leaf when I notice two people approaching my feet. I can't see their faces, for the sun is between their heads. They lie down on their backs beside me, both of them, one of them positioned tightly on either side of me; we are three heads in a row. The person on my right, a woman whom I think I must already know from somewhere, rolls her face toward me till her lips are touching my ear. She gigglingly whispers, "Why don't you come spend the day with us? And maybe the night too. You wouldn't have to sleep in a bed if you didn't want to. Felix and I would enjoy it very much if you came."

"Yes!" said the man to my left. He apparently agreed with the woman. "Zole and I would really enjoy that."

Zole and Felix? Familiar names, yes. But—let me think—I remember *Zole* and *Felix* as names that I once assigned to a couple of people. Yow! Understanding comes creeping up on me. These two people lying here scrunched up too close to me for me to clearly make out their faces could be the same two that I once secretly named *Zole* and *Felix*. Then, however, how do they know that I named them Felix and Zole if I never told them that I had named them anything? I push out my lower lip to blow a cup of air up at the leaf on my nose. I am not like Mack March: I don't tell people the name that I have picked for them and then expect them to not only use the name but welcome it wholeheartedly. The names I come up with are temporary and for my use only. People have their own names! At least most people do, I think. The leaf is now covering one of my eyes.

The woman (Zole?) reaches over and takes the leaf from my eye. She kisses my cheek. "That was a no, I take it," she says.

I nod my head.

The man swings one of his large hands over to place it flat on my midsection. He raises the hand and lowers it again, raises the hand and then gently lowers it. That, I take it, was a friendly tap or two goodbye.

+

They left peacefully. Who are those two that they can be so ingenuous with me? I once asked Mack March how he himself would define the word *hell*. "A place where the dead continue to exist," he answered, responding so quickly and simply I was beginning to believe he was a mind reader.

+

Had I thought of it at the time, I would have quickly switched from darkness to light by shooting back at Mack, "Hah! We have only insubstantial proof of a place where the *living* continue to exist." My comment would have been offhand, sardonic, definitely humorous.

But Mack might not have welcomed my switch. He might have squinched up his eyes and in a serious, penetrating voice said something like this. "If the living merely *return* and don't *continue*, who, precisely, does all of the constructing that makes the world appear to be continuous," he would be looking me dead in the eye, "all the constructing for all the millions of people, and animals too I presume, who are not at this moment in your all encompassing presence?"

My "all encompassing presence" is *your* only definition, I would have retorted furtively in a part of me that Mack couldn't hear, knowing all the while that there is no such place.

Naw, Mack wasn't anywhere in there. That was all me talking, talking like a flatlander, someone who resides in a two-dimensional world. Mack would never have said anything like that tripe about "who does all of the constructing." He rarely said that many words in a row. Besides, he would have known who it is.

+

Is that a sign above the door? Is that a door below the sign? Is that *is that*? No, no no! I grab my head between my hands.

Now it's gone again.

I am being stalked by a haunting image of a door waiting for me to pass through it into an unknown enclosed space. I woke up this morning from a dream of this door, and this phantom door has kept popping up unexpectedly, suddenly before me ever since. This last time was a little different, though. The door had a sign hanging above it. But whatever was written on the sign was either in some very foreign language or it was just a bunch of decorations in a row. So far, the door has always been no longer *there* as soon as it has thoroughly discombobulated me (see above).

Oh! Excuse me if I seemed to be paying no attention for a few minutes there. I was decoding the sign above the door. The sign hung for a while in my memory after it and the door had vanished from before my eyes. The sign is gone from my inner sight too now, and has been ever since I figured out what it said. Here is what I made of the sign: "I tell you, yes, see I you. You are easy to be seen as you. If I see you, are you waning? You!" What does it mean? That—as people used to say all the time—I haven't figured out yet.

I don't expect the door will visit me again now that I have figured the message. Or, maybe the door will return but not the sign. Or maybe the door will return with the sign bearing an easier to read translation of the message. Or maybe the sign will return without the door. The sign will then be blank. It will be looming up before me all shiny like silver and transparent like glass. As I already know the message, I will freely enter the sign. For the sign is a door, undoubtedly the same door. Or, maybe, instead of just incautiously stepping into the sign, I would send in a probe first, someone who just happens to come walking by. From a position of relative safety, I will watch this person go stumbling into the sign. Zap! Crap! Map!

+

"I will return, if not now, sometime, if not sometime, maybe not ever."

Yes, I said that out loud even though there is no one around. No human, that is. I'm thinking this morning of taking down "the curtain." That's what someone called the world yesterday afternoon. This someone was walking past me while talking with someone else, and he (I think it was a *he*) referred to the world as "the curtain." If I take down the curtain, will *it* be black (no light) on the other side, or will *it* be white (all of the lights)? Woops! If I take down the curtain, obviously there won't be any "other side" any longer. Does that mean that *its* being white or black, or a striking combination of the two, is completely my choice? In other words, is my perception of infinity totally dependent on my attitude/training?

You might have noticed the word *infinity* in that last ¶. I don't usually use tacky words like that. I should have said BOUNDLESSNESS. Infinity just writhed its way into that sentence. But boundlessness is a bit hard to swallow, in more ways than one. Given this, given that, I'll leave it as infinity.

-5-

CITY BLACK, BROKEN BACK, SIX STRAWS TO THE WIND

"Amen."

White pants? White shoes! White shirt, white eyes, toast-brown hair. Green eyes. I know I said "white eyes" first, but there's green in there too, sort of an astral green. Yes, I'm aware the stars don't appear to be green except under certain unusual conditions. What was that word he said? "Amen"? Sounds like an old, perhaps prehistoric, word. The way the man used it made the word seem to mean "yes" or "to be sure" or "I agree wholeheartedly." (My proposing the phrase *I agree wholeheartedly* makes me remember that fellow I christened Felix. He said that exact phrase to me twice, once each of the two times I can remember meeting him. But maybe he whom I labeled Felix only to myself but who was also called that to my face by the woman who's maybe always with him—maybe this Felix has been repeating that short string of words at me for eons. And has this new guy here come onstage to sing in the background, "Amen"?) Now he's walking around me, saying that word *amen* twice again, as if he's trying to enclose me in a circle of agreement. He's carefully not looking me in the eyes. Felix would never look me in the eye, either. I'm afraid this man here is not a man but a giant feline, a cougar or jaguar or panther. A panther. He's not a tree, because he's coming at me, not me at him, though trees do move on their own if given sufficient motivation. I used to know a pine tree who would toss a cone at my feet whenever I

66

came into range. But the saw got the tree. Is this man going to get me? What does he want? He has his hand reached way out in front of him like a sword.

He wants to shake hands is what he wants. Felix shook my hand, too. Perhaps this is Felix's brother. Or his clone. Except for those white shoes.

Boy! That was a manly handshake if I've ever experienced one. He nearly crushed my knuckles. He was acting friendly, though, not being a hateful showoff. Is it possible that he could really be that strong, so strong that he wouldn't even know it if he broke my hand into a thousand pieces? A panther might be that strong. A tree definitely could be that strong. I don't know about any of the fishes. Hah! Fishes don't have limbs. I am gazing down at his hands, while he is saying that word. I think I am supposed to be convinced of something. His voice is a voice I remember; I remember this voice from long ago. But I have no memory of this man. Not just his voice, everything about him is as smooth and irresistible as water flowing suddenly over a weir.

What am I going to call this hombre? Assuming he doesn't introduce himself. *Amen.* Yes, that sounds like an apropos name. Amen, as in Amen Ass.

He shook my hand, didn't he? Isn't one supposed to offer his name when he shakes the hand of someone he doesn't know? Could this person think that he *does* know me? His voice is familiar, but his face? No, his face and I have never met. That does not mean, however, that he does not think he already knows me. Sure, Madeleine said she recognized me instantly. And then she said to me before I split in fright, "If you don't help me, I will surely die." Does this man want or expect me to save him from something?

Then Amen says to me, "You don't remember me, do you?" He lays his head way over to one side. "We met some five years ago. It was in a hotel that I don't honestly remember the name of right this minute. But it was big and old and very grand. You read that day to an audience of three to four hundred people, all very grand people, making quite an impression on everyone there. I rushed up to you after the reading, and we shook hands, just like we just did. And I told you my name, Almon Ash. You, you repeated it, my name, over and over, as if it were a mantra. Almon Ash! Almon Ash! Almon Ash! You walked away, repeating my name, and left the hotel, never to be heard of again by anyone I know." His face is one big grin.

I don't ask him who he thinks I am, what he thinks my name is. I don't ask him what it was that he thinks I read from that day five years ago. I do not ask him why he thought I would agree to go inside a building. I will insist instead that he must have made a mistake.

I tell him politely, "No offense intended. But I am certain you have taken me for someone else."

"Not a chance!" he tells me right back. "There is no one else in the WholeWideWorld who looks like you. No one!"

Is he saying he can see that I am green, that I am a green avatar? I don't imagine so. He is more likely only saying that I look out of the ordinary to him. If someone were to ask me what I think I look like, I would not tell them that I think I look unusual. But now that I think about it, neither could I say that I think I look like everybody else.

I have to fight him off, Almon. But even that

doesn't work. So I freeze. I don't look at anything, don't move a muscle, including the ear muscles. I ponder inertia and kinetic energy. I consider 3187 and then 29795. Finally, I take a deep breath and look around me. The man is gone. So is the day. The sun is well down and what light is left is dissolving whimperlessly in the soup of night. Just as I will dissolve whimperlessly in the soup of night.

+

Music. And the sounds of people's voices. Are the sounds coming closer, or is my head clearing of sleep so that I can hear better?

I take my time deciding whether it is worth my time to investigate these noises.

I decree that I will go immediately back to sleep.

I'm riding on a saddleless donkey who's plodding along a dusty trail. Bright sun, no breeze, no arresting smells. The donkey is grey. (Aren't all asses of all breeds some value or values of grey?) The donkey swings her head around to gaze at her passenger. (Are there *she* and *he* donkeys? There must be. I think it's only mules that have their sexuality screwed up. Think! Yes! There *are* girls and boys in the donkey world, Jenny and Jack.) Jenny says to me, "Is it my turn to ride you yet?" Of course I think her request is too quaint, for she can no more ride me than I can ride her anywhere but in my dream.

So the dream is over. It's time to wake up. I wake up, look out the window and down into the park. I'm a statue of a human sitting up in bed and looking out a broad, tall, woodcased window at the greenery across the street.

Below the window stands a woman waiting at a bus stop. Across the street, someone is up in a tree apparently watching the woman.

I am walking along the edge of a small lake. I see someone lying on the grass with one arm stretched out so that the hand is in the water. "Next morning, however, I was sure it had been a dream."

Next morning I am sure it has all been a dream. But I'm up. I'm up for a fresh start. Born again. I am astride a giant cloud, and out of the cloud forms a world. And out of the world forms a dream. And out of the dream forms me. I take on a name, take on a body, take on an identity. I am Rose, a bush of renown that produces celebrated flowers, the most red of flowers spotted with a heavenly yellow. I spread my limbs under my brilliant sun. Given a choice, this is the choice I made.

Next morning I am sure it has all been a dream. But I'm up, up on my feet, up for a fresh start on a new day with a new set of adventures waiting for me.

At least part of the time I seem to be human. Yet why…why don't I get involved like other people do? I can't even decide what gender I'm supposed to be. Everyone else seems to be one or the other or a mix of the two. But me? No, I don't seem to be anything. Oh, people sometimes relate to me as if I'm something or the other. But not really. Their eyes never reach me. Their touch is remote. They name me, I name them. They walk away, or I walk away.

Next morning I am sure it has all been real. I get dirt in my mouth. I can't get my socks on. There's a line of ants marching up my arm.

What am I waiting for? What am I avoiding? "It is

in the nature of the beast," someone said some time or another, "to hesitate." How big can a piece of time get and still be a hesitation?

That was supposed to be a joke, that last question. Pretty flaccid, huh? Suppose I say something else that's not particularly funny. Suppose I say something about reproduction, something that the ants crawling up my arm remind me of. Or, on the other hand (or arm), suppose I don't. Suppose I don't say anything more.

The music and the voices that almost woke me up last night…or was it early this morning? It was so real it could have been absolutely anything.

+

"I'm so real I can be absolutely anything. Make a mark on my forehead, and you'll see what I mean."

There's no room to quibble: this woman is green. Greener than the trees, greener than the grass. It's body paint! Paint has been smeared all over her face, bald head, and naked body. She is so well covered with emerald green paint I can't tell the real color of her skin. If I make a mark on her forehead as she suggested, perhaps by scribing a vertical line with my fingernail, will her skin color show through? Or will she swiftly strike me one-two with her quivering green hands. Her eyes are deep brown. She's smaller than me, shorter with less padding.

She steps closer. She's so close now that I can feel her hot breath on my face. Onions and potatoes and chilies? "Say something!" she says to me.

I try to sound amiable. "What would you like to

discuss?"

"Tell me your name."

"No."

"Then tell me my name."

When I open my mouth to laugh at her request/order, I am surprised to hear myself saying her name, not a name I have made up, her name. "Mimi Reams."

"Thank you," is all she says in return.

She turns around and is walking away from me on the sandy path when I call, "Why do I know your name? Why did you know that I know your name?"

Mimi Reams stops, turns back to face me, and merely smiles. Even in the green paint she is pretty.

I approach her and stand as close as she had stood to me. (What have I had most recently to eat?) "Why don't you answer me, Mimi?"

"It is important that you find your answer yourself."

"If you won't answer me," I quickly say and then repeat the command that she gave me, "say something!"

The woman strokes her hairless green head. "When you can tell me your name, then we will talk." Again she gracefully walks away up the path. But this time she doesn't stop, even when I call her name.

I drop to my knees to say.

My left knee lands on a random rock on the sand of the path, and the rock/knee collision produces a violent white stroke of lightning that shoots from my kneecap up through my thigh and along my backbone to the back of my neck, where it spreads like a giant river delta over the inside of my skull. I fall over onto my side and roll down the path like a lost wiener. I roll right up against someone's feet.

"Strangest snowball I ever saw!" says the head above the feet. "Yet when I look around me, there's no other snow about. So this must be not a snowball at all. Oh ho ho, now I reckon I understand. It's a lone log on a long trip. But a trip to where from where is what I would like to know."

"Hello, Mack."

"Hello, Ial. I've been looking for you."

"What for?" I don't know whether to feel complimented or afraid.

"For two things, Ial." Mack steps back and glances around. "First, I have two bags of brunch, one for you, one for me." He goes over and sits down on the largest of three stones clumped together picturesquely. He's got a one-handed grip on two bulging paper bags.

What do I do first? Am I supposed to ask right now what is the second reason he for looking for me, or am I to sit and eat and enjoy his company and then he will tell me number two?

Mack pats the rock beside him. I get up from the ground and slug over to the rock and sit down.

"Nice pants, Mr. M.," I say sheepishly. He is wearing a wowing pair of brown, black, and cream striped pants. The pleated pants fit him a tad shortly. His roughhewn ankles show between the pant's cuffs and his old mahogany wing tips.

"Yes, a gift from the governor."

I'm totally taken aback. "You just got out of prison?"

"Not that governor." He winks at me, then crosses

his arms over his chest. "'A gift from the governor' is oldtime talk, slave talk. It's referring to someone who thinks they are better off than me."

"Slave talk?"

"A chap I once hung around with claimed he was a slave in his younger days."

"He must have been impossibly old."

Mack hands me one of the bags. "No, he wasn't any older than me. I think he just had an impossibly weird family life."

"*Family* is an unexpected word to hear coming from your mouth."

He laughs. "You didn't know I had it in me, huh?"

"Right."

He laughs again. "I hope that's not the only thing you don't know about me."

He used the word *thing*. So I will use the word *thing*. "What is the other thing? You said you have been looking for me for two things, Mack. First is to share this food with me, you said. Second is what?"

Mack sets his paper bag on the unoccupied stone and strikes a pensive pose. "I've had people come up to me," he says gravely, "people I would not ever have met otherwise. They each and all walked up to me as if they owned the world. They asked me about you." His next sentence he has a hard time saying. "Their questions were worded in such a way that I think they thought you don't live out here, you live somewhere else." He lays his hand on my hurt knee. It stops hurting. "Is it true?" he asks. "Do you live elsewhere?"

I shoot back at him, "Not a chance!"

Mack picks up his bag and opens it, but then he sits quietly waiting.

"How did you figure they were asking about me, Mack? What name did they use for me?"

"No name, Ial. They just described you to me. You are not that hard to unmistakably describe."

Haven't I recently heard something else that smells like that? Yes, but I had better avoid ruminating on it while I'm having company. "Are you making fun of me, mister?"

"The answer to that question is probably a no, maybe a yes, could be a could be. But being as you are getting yourself all riled up at the slim chance that I am poking fun at you, Ial, I will respond with a very definite and emphatic yes."

What will happen if I turn my head squarely toward Mack and stare into his eyes? See! He won't look me straight in the eye, either. His eyes never quite reach my eyes. They always stop, never go any higher than my cheeks and nose—except maybe in my fantasies. I have taken this *habit* of his for the bashfulness of the heroic male type, but in truth he is no different from anyone else. Cat the cat would look right at me!

+

I will read out loud the handwritten note stuck to the tall wooden pole. "I drug the rug, gave it a tug, hug, bug, shrug. I dug the rug. —Signed: THE MUSIC MAN COMETH!" The note is so stupid I have to laugh.

Imitating Mack that time he took down a sign and kept it, I carefully free the paper from the pole and fold it up and stuff it into my pocket. Gotcha! (That's a word Mack uses—*gotcha*.)

It wasn't as hard getting away from Mack this time. I just held Cat's blessed gaze in my mind and got up from the stone and walked away. M.M. didn't say a word that I heard. And I didn't look back. I was and am fairly certain he wasn't going to tell me anything more of use about the people who are out either looking for me or gathering information about me. Which brings to mind again Mimi Reams, the woman in green paint. Is she one of those people? And don't I know of other people, too, who might be *one of them?* Am I one of them?

Am I one of them? Are you one of them? Are we all them? Interesting question: "Are we all them?" Of course you will counter with "Is anyone them?" And I will foolishly say, "Is anyone anyone?" And you will brilliantly respond, "Is anyone?" And I end our mindblasting conversation by saying, "Is?" Or you could then start off in the opposite direction with "Is is?"

So what do I want with that note from off the pole? I've put notes in one or another of my pockets before. And I've left them in there for very long periods. When finally I take them out, they are always deeply saturated with the smells of history, with the time and distances of the world. Everything is recorded in there. I could go to any city anywhere and never get lost. I could swim down to the bottom of the ocean and not drown, if I didn't lose the note along the way. So! I thought it was about time to start another essence collector in my pocket.

Someone is walking speedily toward me with a glint in his eye. I hope he is not the composer and once-owner of the note in my pocket. Will I defend my right to take down the piece of paper and keep it as my own? How long does a posterhanger have to be away from his poster for the poster to become public property? Has this question ever been addressed?

Mr. Glint-in-the-eye strides right on by me, doesn't even throw me a glance, totally ignores me, gives me zip for encouragement, could have been on another planet altogether! "Hear me! He could have been on another planet altogether!"

What am I doing, shouting aloud at no one? When I first saw the man coming, I was afraid he was going to give me a load of crap—but as soon as I was sure he was not going to do that, I got angry with him for not doing that. How terribly terrible of me. How terribly terribly terribly terrible of me.

"I beg your pardon. Were you speaking to us, Jolty?"

Ah-h-oh! Who's behind me?

Around I spin, and I see a little man and a little woman standing there arm in arm, gazing blissfully up at my eyes—looking me right smack-dab in the eyes. Very old they are, wrapped in silvery grey.

"It's so nice to see you, Jolty."

The man said that.

"It's just lovely to see you again, Jolty."

The woman said that.

"Who is this *Jolty*?" It is me who said that.

Yes, yes, yes, you're right, it's time to let it out. This *Jolty* they spoke of could be me. Jolty Jone is the name, a name I haven't used for a long time, a name that I sometimes remember, oftentimes don't, but never use. And now you know it, my name. And now, I suppose, you will always be reminding me of it whenever I forget. That is why I didn't tell you my name before: I want to be able to forget, forget the name and the identity that goes with the name. Without a name and a pat identity, my world is both infinitely larger and infinitely smaller; it's boundless yet totally simple. I would laugh and say that I want to be free, but we all know what freedom is. So I won't use that word again.

"*You* are Jolty, our only child." The man said that. There is just a touch of worry showing behind his gladness to see me.

"Jolty, my Jolty!" The woman said that. There is no worry to be seen in her, only happiness.

What can I do? I just stand there staring back at them. They know my name, my first name anyway; but I do not know them. We have never before met.

No, contrary to appearances I am not using that old tactic: If it looks like you're losing the game, deny that you're playing. I really and truly do not know these people. I don't know them now, I did not know them when they were younger. They are strangers to me.

They step near to me. The man lays his hand on my coupled hands. The woman comes to the side of me and hugs my upper arm. Who are they and what do they want? I seem to be asking that question every thirty seconds or so. Who are they and what do they want?

Who are they and what do they want?

I can't just stand like a frozen piece of meat again.

I'll have to make a run for it. Old as they are, I might be able to outrun them.

6

JOCKO

Jolty Jone. There I go, reminding myself and it's not even noon yet. Bad child! *Child?* Strange choice, that word. Ahh, yes, I know exactly where the word came from. I can still see the worried look on that old man's face as he said to me, "Jolty, our only child." Why? I'm not asking here why did he have a worried look on his face or why I can still see it; I am asking why did he say the "our only child" thing. But, yes, why did he have a worried look on his face? And, yes, why can I still see it?

The only thing I can think to do right now to get away from all this…from all this… (I am trying to think of a workable next word. I came up with *unsettledness*, but I don't think it is the word I want. *Mystery* is a possibility. No, *unsettledness* is better than *mystery*. How about *instability?* Or *inconstancy?* No, none of those words has the right ring. Not one of them, except maybe to a limited extent *mystery*, bears the stain of unexpectedness. So why don't I just use that word, *unexpectedness?*) The only thing I can think to do now to get away from all this unexpectedness is to climb a tall, thickly foliated tree and go to sleep or at least close my eyes tightly and keep them closed. But I would have to walk a ways to do that, for none of the trees around here fit the bill.

My mouth drops way way open. I don't believe my ties. Who do I pee coming at me? Why, it's the tree I used to perch in to watch Hossmattcha board her bus.

+

So! Where am I, and what am I doing? I am comfortable up here. I can't see any streets or bus stops, can't see Hossmattcha; but my screaming muscles are relaxing, my mind is drifting naturally, and I feel safe. Mind you, *safe* is a word I'd rather not be remembered as having used that way in a sentence.

Who do I spy standing on the ground below me with arms spread pleadingly and her head laid back so that she can fully gaze up at me? Not Hossmattcha, no. And not Madeleine Phitt again. Not Zole. Not Taxi, since she's long dead. It could be the woman who was lying with a hat covering her face, but I don't know if it is her or not because I never saw that woman's face. I'm certain it's not Mimi Reams, though, because I can remember now what Mimi looked like without the green paint. I can remember? Of course, gool-fool, I says sarcastically to myself. Along with a proper name comes a pat identity. I said my name just a while ago; so I am now remembering the life that went with that name.

Can I stop the memory process? I might be able to trick it into stopping; I doubt I could stop it face on.

I'll pretend I'm dead.

+

It worked.

If I can say that it worked, it didn't work. Right? I'll have to pretend some more.

Dead in a tree.

81

I rise from the dead, climb down from the tree, look around. My mind is clear, untroubled by whatever made me think I was dead.

Have I been reborn? Is it possible that that's all that death is?

7

CERTAINLY

They are riding the eight-ten commuter train. He is sitting facing in the direction the train is traveling. She is sitting in the seat facing his seat. They have not met before, yet they will soon be talking to each other, necessarily talking loudly enough that others will be tempted to listen.

Out of the blue he says, "Your name is written on your arm."

She laughs lightly at his unfamiliar approach. Confident that there is no way he can know her name, she says back to him, "Can you read it to me? I seem to have forgotten it."

"It says," he says with a long pause here in the middle, "Claire Fullblood."

She gasps, shakes her head, sticks the point of her tongue between her lips. "How did you know that?"

"One of my many talents."

Her hands involuntarily jump to the back of her head. She rubs her black hair, then forces her hands to return to her lap. "What can I say? Since it is not one of my talents to see people's names on their arms, you will have to tell me your name."

"Certainly."

Claire waits.

The man waits.

"Well, are you going to tell me?"

The man can't help but grin. "Certainly is my name. Certainly Ridge."

Claire Fullblood wiggles her head in disbelief. "Your first name is actually *Certainly*?"

"It certainly is. How much problem are you going to have with that?"

"Oh, I'll get used to it."

"You are not getting used to it very fast, Claire. You should have said, 'Oh, I'll certainly get used to it, Certainly Ridge.'"

"Where'd you ever pick up a set of names like that? Ridge could be a family name; I might have even heard it before. But I can't remember ever hearing Certainly used as a person's name, first or last."

"I picked them out myself. Not my very first memory, but my second—my second memory was of me asking two questions, and *certainly* was the answer to both of those questions. My third memory was also a question, and *ridge* was the answer to that question."

'You picked out your names? Your parents didn't?"

"Right. I have no memory of parents. Do you have some parents?"

"Of course. Everyone does." Claire fidgets uncomfortably on her seat. "Or, rather, excuse me, I should have said that everyone *does* or *did* have parents." She recovers from her perplexity to say, "And almost everyone has some kind of memory of their parents, even if they never met them. Some kind of memory."

"Very curious it is to me how certain you are of something you have no way of knowing."

Carefully Claire considers Certainly's scarcely concealed offensive. "Yeah, yeah. You're just turning tricky now, Mr. Certainly Ridge. What I told you are facts: that everyone has or had parents and that most everyone has at least a weak memory of their parents. These two facts are unassailable *common knowledge*." She seems to savor her last two words. "They're part of the shared wisdom that every member of our culture has a right to use without fear of attack."

Certainly slowly nods his head at the mouthful Claire has delivered. He grins out the side of his mouth. "And how do you or I tell the difference between shared wisdom and culturally reinforced delusion?"

"Huh?" Claire is momentarily confused by the intent as well as the meaning of his question. She is surprisingly quick to reply. "I'll go you one farther, sir: culture is entirely delusion. But out of this chaos of illusion/delusion an order is formed. And the bones of this order are called wisdom. Wisdom can be sighted from other vantage points as well; but I don't know of nor can I conceive of any whole wisdom that fails to acknowledge biological birth. Hence, there is not only a child, there are always parents in the mix somewhere."

"Are you telling me I'm an alien?" Certainly makes a funny face at her. "An unearthly, unbiologically produced zipzap? Am I supposed to be unnaturally dangerous to fine looking women too?"

Claire stops short. She stares unwaveringly at Certainly's eyes. Then she looks away, at his knee or something. "You have not even the faintest memory of your parents?"

"I have not the faintest memory of anyone who could be called my parent."

"I can see you are being sly and you are putting me

on." Claire has not looked up at Certainly's face. "But are you *only* putting me on? If we are going to continue this conversation till one of us gets off this train, you are going to have to promise me that your answers are the truth."

"I am telling you no lies."

"You said that your second memory was such and such and your third memory was such and such too." Her eyes are rising. "What was your first memory?"

"Climbing down from a tree."

"You! You *are* putting me on!" Claire jerks her head away and glares out the window. She can't see much out there because they have gone underground.

"No, I'm not putting you on. That is my first memory, climbing down from a tree. There is a faint light showing way out in front of that first memory, but it is such a faint light that it's nothing but a dumb glow."

+

He is sitting facing the window. She is sitting with her back to the window, facing him. They are both sitting on very old, green and beige, embroidered chairs. This is her sitting room in her house on her quarter acre of land near the heart of the city. Claire inherited this property. She has changed it only slightly to fit her needs. Certainly gets up from his chair to walk over to an inside wall to admire a small square painting. Reds and greens. Yellows. Blues. Browns. At first the painting seems to show only it's rich colors. Little by little figures become discernible. Poor people lying on deep grass in the sun. One figure—maybe it is a female—has started to stand up. Claire lets out a sharp cry. Certainly spins about to see what her trouble is. Claire sighs and says that that is her most favorite painting in the world. The figure starting to stand up is her. She has spent some time in the tropics. The scene was painted by a man who traveled from village to village. He gave it to her in exchange for one soft kiss on his lips. Certainly turns back to the painting. He can see now that the woman is Claire. Why had he not been able to see that before?

He is sitting in her automobile. He is dressed all in dark blue. She is sitting beside him, looking out the front window (windshield). She doesn't turn on the machine. They get out and return to the house.

+

Claire is coming back from the front door with the food they had called out for when she stops in the middle of the room and says up at the wood ceiling in an unshakable voice, "She cannot love, she is so self-endeared."

Spread out rather randomly on the embroidered chair, the chair he will adopt as his in the room they will adopt as theirs, Certainly asks, "Who cannot love? The delivery person?"

"No, that little excerpt was about no one in particular."

"Excerpt? Were you quoting someone, Claire?"

"I was, though I have no idea who. An old writer, I think."

"Do you think there is any chance you had yourself in mind when you gave voice to that excerpt?"

"Is that what you think of me, that I'm self-endeared?"

"My answer is a flat no." Certainly removes his leg from the arm of the chair. "I was merely asking the question you had made obvious."

"Why would I make it *obvious*, Certainly?"

"You would make it so obvious that I would have to ask it, and you could then ask in reply if that is what I think of you."

Claire's jet hair flies as she brusquely twirls her head. "And we would pick up momentum—right?—till we are spinning round and around each other."

"Righto, Claire."

"What say we just eat instead?"

"Good idea, gal."

They retire to the smallish carved-oak table in the bay window. Actually the room has two bay windows. One overlooks the colorful garden at the side of the house. And Claire and Certainly are now sitting side by side, looking out the other five-paneled window, looking out through pale sheers at the green front yard, the grey iron fence, the white sidewalk and black street. The table would seat four people comfortably, two on either side. Even so, it was probably not intended to be used as a dining table.

"While you've got that food in your mouth, answer me this, Certainly. You got off the train at my stop. You followed me everywhere I went. You followed me to work and sat outside my office until I gave up and left with you."

"That is correct. But are you asking me a question?"

"Relax. The question is forthcoming." Claire picks up a morsel of the whatever-it-is food with her fingers and puts it in her mouth. She chews the bite, swallows it, and licks the tips of her fingers. "Where would you have gotten off the train if we hadn't talked?"

"At the same place. And I would have followed you everywhere that you went, just like I did."

"No! You're misunderstanding me, Certainly. I appreciate the compliment, if it was one; but what I am asking here is where do you usually get off. What is your normal destination?"

"I have no normal destination. This morning was my first trip on the train. I am a newborn child in your hands."

Claire laughs loudly. She has to cover her mouth with her hand. She inadvertently knocks her throwaway fork off the table. "No, I'm not not not telling you that you're an alien, Mr. Ridge!"

+

Late afternoon fell into a deep evening and that evening into night, a night that might have lasted forever had not Certainly gotten up from the silk sheets that Claire is so fond of and collided with a wall in the dark. Claire heard the sound of a body hitting her bedroom wall and thought that vigilantes had arrived to hang her the way blackmasked ruffians hanged her grandfather. Unsheeted by Certainly's exit, she floated above the bed in fright. Certainly corrected what damage to his person he could correct in the dark and returned to the bed, because Claire was moaning. Claire was moaning as softly as a lone desert cloud in the moonlight.

Certainly stands over the bed gazing down at Claire. He cannot see that her eyes are tightly closed. Except for her dark hair, she is a silver coin at the bottom of the pond.

+

Her dark hair? Except for her dark hair she is a silver coin. She moans like a lone desert cloud, she inherited the house and grounds, her grandfather was hanged, she corrected herself when she said that everyone has parents, she is maybe not certain she can love.

They seldom leave the house. They seldom leave their room. They buy some paints and begin painting giant scenes on the walls. They paint around the small square tropical painting, leaving a two foot band of unpainted wall above and below and on both its sides. Sometimes they work together on a section of wall; sometimes they work by themselves. When they work together, they work as one. When they work separately, their paintings always mesh magically without a visible seam. And they laugh a lot.

Yes, they laugh when they are together. Yet Claire awakens each morning before sunrise, quietly takes herself out in her dressing gown to the "servants stoop" on the other side of the house than the garden, sits down on the top step, and cries. She cries silent, bowling-ball tears. Certainly knows she does this, and he doesn't interfere. He waits till the tears stop and her face dries before he goes out himself to join her on the stoop. He is usually packing two naked pieces of toast with him for them to munch on while watching the sun rise.

They make silent friends with the few people they

see the few times they go out, away from the house. Everyone remembers them and greets them the next time they see them.

The first outsider to actually engage Claire and Certainly in conversation is a daring musician/composer who takes a liking to them and asks them to come, visit his studio. The next (and last) forward person is a fearless playwright who invites them to coffee and chat at her favorite café. Claire and Certainly enjoy the café and start going there themselves each morning after Claire has had her cry. One such morning, they are making their trek to the café when the musician spots them on the street and rushes to their side to present them with a tune he has written for them. Yes! They thank him. Minutes later in the café, Claire and Certainly are humming the tune when the playwright hears them from another table and comes over to their table. Curious, she inquires about the tune. Claire and Certainly tell her about the music and, to a limited extent, about themselves. The playwright is thinking long and deeply about what they have said when, all at once, she breaks into her greatest smile and begs Claire and Certainly to write a song to go with the music. She will use it in her play, she says, the play currently being performed locally, twice weekly. That night, Claire and Certainly go in disguise to see the play. On their way back home they discuss the play and are certain the production has no place in it for their song. Be that as it may, they rise to the challenge and write the song, inserting here and there bright points from their life together, especially their first meeting on the train. The audiences love the song. Claire and Certainly are asked to write more songs, but they decline. They stop going to the café.

The following Monday morning, Claire returns to work. That is to say she takes herself to her office with the intent to work at her job. Certainly accompanies her on the train. It's the second time he has ridden the train. From the station they walk hand in hand in a light rain to the tall sea-green building. Inside the building, at her office door Claire gives Certainly a damp peck on his lips. Certainly promptly goes over and sits down again on the same chair outside her office to wait. Claire waves goodbye at him and disappears behind the door. But a couple of hours later, when Claire comes out to ask Certainly if he would like a tour of her floor, the chair is empty. Certainly is nowhere to be seen. He is not there. Claire remains standing on that one spot just outside her door for a full minute. Suddenly she shouts in a screeching voice to a group of passersby, "Either someone has stolen him or he has climbed back up in his tree."

-8-

CLAIRE

Claire. Someone aims their hurricane at her, and she splatters so hard against the brick wall she feels every bone in her body break. That doesn't matter to her too much because her head hits the wall with an outrageous tree-cracking sound and she knows she will die immediately. Whether she lives or dies, the whole back of her body will soon be one big purple flame.

She gets up from her bed and shuffles barefoot/barebody into the bathroom to sit on the toilet in the dark. She rubs up and down her thighs with just the palms of her hands. Certainly did that to her thighs once while she was sitting on this stool. He was down on his knees before her.

Slipping mindlessly into a dressing gown while deliberately not turning on any of the lights in the house, Claire stumbles out through the laundry room to sit on her crying porch. Why did she call this little porch "the servants stoop" all her life? She only stopped calling it that after Certainly has come and gone. There hasn't been a single domestic employed in this house since before Claire was born. There is *no one* in the house now, she says to herself. That is only too true, but that truth will dissolve the next day.

Early the next morning she is sitting in the café sipping hot sauce and glancing through the morning's paper. She has about twenty-five minutes to waste before she catches her train to work. Her coming to the café surprised her.

The playwright watches out the side of her eyes and sort of waves when Claire waves at her. Neither of them get up and saunter over to the other's table. Claire presses back her hair with both her hands. "The very first thing she'd ask me is where is Certainly."

The fellow at the next table leans toward her, smiling. "I beg your pardon. I didn't hear what you said."

Claire's lips curl up in scorn. "You weren't supposed to."

Grunting impolitely, the man directs his chair away from her.

I am certainly not making new friends too fast. This time Claire isn't speaking out loud. *I've had all of my life to make friends, but here I am. I don't think I am at all unpleasant to look at. And my teeth are clean and white. So? Am I here all alone because I just don't have anything to say to anyone? Maybe I am an empty vessel.* Claire laughs, and several sleepy heads bounce up to see what's happening. Remembering all that talking, hours and hours of it, that she did with Certainly, Claire cackles loudly.

The man from the next table, the fellow Claire insulted, boards the same train and sits in the seat that faces hers. Claire tries ignoring him, tries pouting at him, tries smiling at him.

He grins back. "Am I forgiven, madam?"

"Yes, indeed you are. And I apologize for my gruffness, sir."

The man stands halfway up, puts out his hand, says his name. "Near Moss."

Claire can't believe her ears. *A guy named Certainly*

Ridge sits across from me on the train and then a guy named Near Moss! The man sits back down, jams his untaken hand into his lap. But before his grin has completely dissolved, Claire says her name.

The man seems confused by Claire's last name. "Ahh…Fullblood?"

I guess I had that coming. Claire puts out her hand to him. "Do you go to the café often?"

"No." The man is truthful. He takes her hand and shakes it lightly, warmly. "Today was my first time in a café, Claire." He stressed the word *café*. "I seem to be of a different order than the people who spend time in such places. No offense intended, please."

No offense intended? Is he saying he can see that I am green? Claire giggles. "Now that was a strange thought."

The man, Near, laughs at her pleasure. "Tell me."

"I just had the thought that you said what you said because you can see that I am green."

"You're green at what, Claire?"

"At what?" Claire doesn't understand his question at first because he is using a different meaning of *green* than she was. She picks up on his definition and quickly answers accordingly. "Green at hanging out at cafés. Me too."

Before Claire gets off the train (Near is to get off at the next stop), they arrange to meet and have lunch together in the park. And some hours later, there in the park, they arrange to have dinner together and to take in a show of some kind afterwards. Near is to come to Claire's house. From there they will walk to an area with lots of restaurants and then choose the place that appeals to them.

Near rings the doorbell. It's six-thirty-ish. He's right

on time. Claire lets him in. She isn't dressed yet. Would he like to wait in the "giant scenes" room? Near and Claire know they are not going to leave the house. Evening falls into a deep night, and that night into a glorious Saturday morning.

"Nork, nork, the maverick snorts."

Near throws back the covers to let the sunlight that's coming down through the skylight land on his body. "What are you going on about, Claire? What's a *nork*?"

He is certainly hairier than Certainly. Claire kicks her covers clear off the bed. "I was just verbalizing free associations." She slaps the tight skin of her tummy. "A meaning might be thereby produced, but usually it's not. Rhyming is not important, Near, yet near-rhyming usually occurs. *Nork* is nothing in particular."

Near straightens out his dong, limp now after its last, quite recent visit to Claire's donga. His dong, her donga. "I'm not much on fancy word usage, Clairest. Does your 'verbalizing free associations' have a different effect on you than, say, finding that you have switched words around without planning to? Take for example this sentence: 'She could feel every body in her bone break.' Hmm?"

Wow! That quiets Claire right down. She remembers the feeling of every bone of hers breaking in the dream she had two nights before. *Near Moss has picked something out of my nigh terminal dream, turned it into a flip plaything, and given it back to me. Is he an amateur, or does he know well what he is doing?*

"You've turned deathly still, Claire. Did I say something that offended you?"

"Did I talk in my sleep last night?"

"Just once, for maybe thirty seconds, I could hear

the air moving in and out of your nose. Otherwise you slept perfectly quiet all night. I actually checked your pulse once to make sure you were still aboard."

"I didn't say anything about a dream?"

Near shakes his head no.

Claire works her lips over and under each other. "Your example sentence, without the word switching, is right out of my dream from two nights ago."

"My example sentence, without the word switching, is right out of the newspaper two mornings ago. It was the biggest headline on the front page of the second section."

Wow! That quiets Claire right down. *I'm going to have to be more careful with this guy. He's not as uncomplicated as he looks.*

+

Dead? What does that mean? Who *is* that woman standing on the ground below pleading up at me? Yellow. I will climb down from this tree. Ugh! I *can't* climb down from the tree! Yellow? If I can say that it worked, it didn't work. Right? I feel like I'm caught between two big rivers. I'll have to pretend some more.

Dead in a tree.

+

"Outshine!"

"What are you meaning this time? *Outshine?* Is that another nothing-in-particular like *nork*, Claire?"

"I'm meaning we should get out of bed, dear Near."

Where can I find a two-day-old newspaper without going into a library? "We should take a shower and dress ourselves. And then—this is the crux of the meaning—we should transport our lights out of this house to shine ever so brightly in the outer world." Claire sweeps her fingers, four on each side, lightly over her cheeks from her mouth to her ears. "And I shalt not forget that while we are out there shining we might see if we can find us a Saturday's breakfast-at-noon to fill in the holes left by our not going out to dinner last night."

Near rolls over on his belly and hooks his chin on Claire's shoulder. "And while we are out there searching for this phantom-like late breakfast, we will walk in the bright sunlight, holding hands, smiling at everyone we pass like two big idiots."

"I think you have pretty well got the idea now, lennie."

"Lennie?"

"I thought *lennie* would sound better than *laddie*, which first came to mind. But now neither word is especially pleasing. So I will revert to *Near.*"

"Thank you. I appreciate your reversion."

It takes longer than either of them might have expected to get out of the house: more sex, wild games in the shower, etc. It is nearly two in the afternoon before they hit the concrete. Claire, thinking she is going to have to direct their moves, calls the first three turns herself. Near just nods his head at each corner.

But when Claire points her index finger for the fourth time, Near shakes his head and says without an smidgen of self-doubt, "No, let's go that thataway."

They go thataway. Near calls the following two

turns and comes to a halt before a three-story brick building. He points at the third floor. "That is where I live."

Claire points at the first floor. "What is that?"

"That, Claire, is a restaurant. If they don't serve breakfast in there at this hour, which I think they don't, I'm sure they will if I ask them to."

So it's restaurants for this guy instead of cafés? "It doesn't look much like a restaurant to me."

"It's not actually a restaurant."

"What is it then?"

"Well, actually, it's a restaurant."

"Are you going to show me your abode up there before we eat?"

"No, let's eat first. I'm starving, and my place is a mess."

What a mess! What is a mess? Everyone's definition of a mess must be different. I've never ever see a home neater than this, no home that still looks lived in.

The restaurant below had fixed "Near and his friend anything they want to eat." They even sent a young man rushing out to the store for sprouts. Claire was impressed. She asked Near if he is related to the people who run the establishment. He said, no, he just eats here frequently.

"I like your place Mr. Moss."

They have climbed the stairs to Near's apartment and are now standing just inside the door, looking around. Claire is suddenly feeling like a normal person. This is scaring her. *Good sex, good talk, good frolicking, good stroll, good food, a visit to the male's apartment—how normal can one get?* Obviously Claire thinks that her life up till now has not been ordinary. She spins about, descends the stairs, and walks at a good pace back to her house.

Near follows a half block behind her. She slams and locks her front door before he gets there. He knocks softly. He knocks again. He is about to knock a third time when he hears the lock in the door turning.

Near moves in with Claire. He doesn't exactly move in. He packs over a suitcase of clothes and a box of miscellaneous. (Near does not own an automobile and probably isn't aware that Claire has one in her garage. He has not yet been in the garage.)

+

Claire still gets up in the morning before sunup. She checks in the dim light to see if Near is sleeping, then takes herself out to her crying porch. She doesn't cry out there anymore; she just sits and waits for the sun with her arms wrapped around her knees. As far as she knows, Near has never noticed that she leaves the bed every morning. He's still asleep when she returns. But! She reminds herself again and again that he is not as plain as he wants people to think he is.

They go every morning to that same café where they met. The playwright secretly watches them, but no one else pays them any mind. They eat, drink, read, and leave to catch the train to work.

They join up again for lunch in the park. And they meet in the train station in the evening to walk to the restaurant under Near's apartment. Claire has never again gone up to his apartment. They just eat and then walk slowly to her house.

Early one morning, when Claire goes out to her porch, Certainly is sitting on the step where she usually sits. He scoots over a bit, and she sits down beside him. He doesn't say anything; he simply looks off at the point between two buildings where the sun will make its entry.

Claire stares at the side of his face. This is the morning that restarts her crying. "Where you been, boy?"

Certainly smiles but still doesn't look at her. He gets up from the step and leaves without having said a single word.

The next time Claire sees him, she's sitting next to Near on the train. Claire and Near get on the train and sit down and there he is, Certainly, sitting in the seat facing them, looking out the window. He looks out that window the whole trip. And when Claire and Near get up to get off, Certainly is still staring out the window.

Claire hopes Certainly will be on the evening train too. He isn't. She is expecting him the next morning; but, again, he is nowhere to be seen on the train.

That evening, when Claire and Near walk into their restaurant, Certainly is sitting at the table next to the one always reserved for them. They sit down, he gets up to leave.

She looks and looks for him, but that was the last time Claire sees Certainly. It's not the last time that day or that week or that year, it's the last time ever in her life, which doesn't go on much longer. Claire's life that is. She hands over the keys to her property to Near and goes in search of Certainly's tree, the one he remembers climbing down from. Soon she is dead.

From who knows what.

Before she dies she does find an occupied tree. Regrettably, the tree is not occupied by Certainly. Who *is* that woman standing on the ground below pleading up at me?

SKYLIGHT DILEMMA UTILITY

So the dream is over. I'm sure it has been but a dream; there has to be more, or less, to death than that; that was way too simple, while much too complex. So? So I'll get down from here now. Hold it! Should I take my name down with me or leave it up here in the tree to flower in the sun? That one is a hard decision to make, a skylight dilemma. I will...uh...take it along! Yes! Jolty Jone is climbing down from this tree, ho-ho. Jolty Jone's feet touch the earth, hee-hee. The difference runs deeper than the color.

Yikes! I no more than had both of my feet solidly on the ground when a thought—or something quite alien that looks and feels believably similar to a thought— suddenly popped up on my screen: *Knowing only his own, individual mode of being, Doormouse is given to believe he is very old in the scheme of things.* From whence cometh a file of scrap like that? Look out! Here comes another one! *Coarse republican blood coursing through their bodies.* From where-o-where, do tell me, did that scarlet flag fly here? And here's yet another one! This one's even more juvenile and cryptic than the first two. *Dark matter plunging though the universe.*

I wanted to say *juvenilely cryptic* instead of *juvenile and cryptic,* but to the best of my memory the word *juvenile* does not have a recognized adverb form. Or would that be...does not have a *recognizable* adverb form. Either way, either way. If I am in error on this adverbial matter, please let me know. I will repay you with a beautiful adjective gesture. If not sooner.

I take pause. Should I allow the aforementioned opaque "thoughts" to escape into the outer world, or should I keep the tenebrous threesome all to myself? Is there anyone handy hereabouts to whom I could let them out if I decide to let them out? I'm looking around. No, I appear to be all alone here. Not counting you, of course. I could perhaps go and relay the terrible three to that beat-up, lonely garbage can over there. No, I get no satisfaction (to speak of) from talking out loud in words to anything other than humans and humanized animals, which includes untamed birds in cages.

Right, I'm remembering that marvelous raven, the one penned up in an overly strong cage. The way he stared at me that day reminds me of my staring at you this minute of this day, which reminds me that if I am to eventually become like you and occupy everything and be everywhere, I will have to stand comfortably everywhere. That is, I will have to stand comfortably even on the points of opinion that I don't agree with. That is all too obvious, is it not, as obvious as the fact that you are everywhere I look?

Woo! Talking about you gives me the willies. I'd better get my jomo-jomo working here. Maybe then I could get one sly genius at work here. Maybe then I could remember where I went while I was dead.

I might also remember the last time that I had something to eat. Something other than the air in my nose and the dew on my lips. Maybe ol' Mack March will just happen by with another bag of muffins. Woo! I'd better be careful here: Thinking in this manner about a desire (hunger in this case) almost always produces a direct result all right, but the result is usually way too far off to the side to be of any use in quenching the desire, to say the least. I just hope it isn't Madeleine Phitt who draws alongside, Madeleine Phitt with a handful of throbs. Though I wouldn't mind a bit seeing Cat again.

Is desire (hunger in this case) the skylight dilemma? I don't truthfully know. I thought the dilemma was simply whether I would take my name with me when I climbed down from the tree, which doesn't seem to me to have anything to do with desire, particularly not with hunger.

Now I have two, opposing thoughts on this skylight dilemma matter. The first is that my hunger will soon pass, taking the desire with it, while my name will haunt me as if forever. The countering thought is that my name will soon fade from view, while desire will be with me as if forever, will be with me until I discover the sunlight dilemma utility.

I have to close my eyes! Annh! Suddenly I'm moving very fast! I can feel my feet and they… They're not moving at all! Naw! The world around me is moving with me! And someone is beside me. I can't see this person or this person's feet, but I know the feet are wearing white socks and white shoes. (Who do I know who wears white shoes?) Not the person beside me, someone in the distance says in a loud voice, "I don't think you want to leave *that* here." How would I know which *that* is that? I still can't open my eyes. I rub my hands up and down over the washboard folds on my forehead. What's that? I just caught sight of something in my internal vision. Now I'm making out a diamond-shaped sign moving rapidly toward me a little off to one side. Black letters on the yellow sign spell out "Paddle Units Which Protrude From The Underneath." The inscrutable sign (it's not acting like a memory) is accompanied by piercing, faster than sound, brilliant white streamers of sound, sound that is as fast as and as visible as lightning, sharp, jagged streamers. I open up my external vision, and everything instantly returns to normalsville.

So what is more normal than asking what is more normal? I guess *more normal* is an ok construction, but it looks funny to me. No more on that later, I hope.

You know, I don't have to stay stuck with a two-word name forever. Plenty of other people have three words in their names, three or even more. Jaunty Jolty Jone. How does that sound? Terrible, huh? Jolty Won Huh Jone. I know, I know; that was no better. Hmm, *Better*. Jolty Jone Better. Well, that is some better. Jolty Jone Some Better. Nope! Stop! Today, I guess, is not the day to add to my name. I will just walk aimlessly for a while.

"Did Claire Fullblood ever check the newspaper for that headline she might have used in her dream?"

I remain cool, exceedingly cool. I was walking along not very fast but fast enough, when words, those words, came from immediately behind me. And I do not hear anyone walking around here but me. If I stop now to investigate, I'll be taking a chance on causing a violent collision. So I'll just keep on walking. Yes, I'll keep on walking because there is no one at all back there behind me.

What I do is cut a big hook to the left and then stop and turn to look. Well bless my knoll! I could have kept on turning around and around till I was spinning like a drill bit and boring my way toward the center of the earth, but I still would not have seen anybody behind me. For there isn't anyone there. No body that I can see anyway.

I'm walking again, not quite so steady of step this

time. Who is this Claire Fullblood? (You might ask why I am assuming that Claire Fullblood is a person or at least a human. Humans go to newspapers for info. That's not a real-tight or perfectly logical answer, I know. It will have to do for the time being, though.) And the voice? The voice, the voice, the voice. I'm concentrating my attention on the voice.

As if in answer, the same voice as before chants behind me, "Near is near. Near is not. Near is not near. Near is near. Near is not."

I'm not going to even look back. That was number two. Is there going to be a third message-of-sorts, like there were three bad bic-bics back under the tree? From where are these "thoughts" coming? They, like the speeding sign, don't act like memory. And they don't have the feel of imagination per se either. I'm not quite the avatar I once was, yet surely I would detect any and all spirit people, visible or not, who got that close to me.

Speaking of *non-visible people*, what does that mean? Everybody I've ever met is invisible right now, I don't see a single person around here. So, hence, therefore, everyone but me is invisible at least most of the time. So everyone but me is a ghost most of the time. Now that was a real-tight and perfectly logical answer to the number one question of perception. You, of course, are necessarily exempt from this proof—I'll call my answer a proof, like scientists do.

That was a nice little mind-trip. It made me forget the voice behind me. And my head is clearer. I seem to be more in the life half of existence now than the death half. I look up at the sun. I call it by name. "Sun!" And again I call out it's one-word name. "Sun!" It answers me with a great wave of warmth. I have to stop walking. I stop and slowly rotate my body so that every part of me gets its share of the sun's warmth. When my energy tanks are refilled, I squirt out a little bit of that energy onto the earth in repayment to the sun.

"Hello there."

Words coming from behind me again! That's number three. Maybe. I say maybe because the words were said in a decidedly different voice this time. There may be in reality a self-starting vessel of flesh and blood standing right behind me. (Someday I will rid my life of its if's and maybe's. Remind me if I forget.)

"Hello again. I was taken with the way you were turning your body. Are you a dancer out here practicing?"

I'm beginning to feel confident that someone is actually back there. What do I do in that case? Lower my arms to my sides, turn around smiling and say a nice hello-in-return to whatever I see standing there, yes? No. I fold my hands behind my head and drop into a deep turning curtsy with an immense grimace on my mug. And I don't say hello. I say, "Well well." I say that because there is no one there where the voice came from, no one standing, sitting, or flying through the air. No one.

How can this be explained? What do you think is going on with me? First I have thoughts that feel as if they are not my thoughts but someone else's. Then I see and hear a highballing sign with my eyes closed. Then I hear a voice behind me talking about people I don't know—if "Near" is a person. And just now there was another voice behind me addressing me, talking directly to me it seemed.

Realizing that all this has occurred in the short

stretch of time since I climbed down from the tree, I'm beginning to think that I got down from on high too fast and the pressure increase bonked me, like someone surfacing too quickly from a great depth of water. Makes sense, doesn't it? Does to me.

I just had a thought: My climbing up into the tree, staying there for a while, and then climbing back down might not have taken an hour, a day, or even a year. A hundred years could have passed! Didn't someone write a story once about a guy who did exactly that? Am I number two?

I get a grip on myself and look here and there and perceive no major changes. I see buildings through the trees; and turning and looking in the other direction, I see through the trees, buildings. But more importantly, neither of these two views strikes me as having changed significantly since I climbed the tree. Everything looks the same. So, hence, therefore, my hundred year sleep probably didn't happen.

"Hello there."

Unh! Words from behind me again! I thought we had already done number three. Isn't number three always the end-all? Or has someone merely turned on REPEAT PLAY?

"Hello again. I was taken with the way you were turning your body. Are you a dancer out here practicing?"

Agh! The exact same ironic-sounding words!

I just had a thought. What if there is indeed someone back there now saying the same two hellos I have already heard? Does that mean that I am nearing my omnipotence? A more likely explanation, I suppose, is that this area's time is cracking open. Does that mean that there is another me somewhere around here asking the same questions?

I stop asking you questions the instant I feel a hand on my shoulder. When the hand slips down my back to my waist, I stop breathing altogether. I-I-I carefully turn around.

Sky-blue eyes. Very very pale skin. Orange freckles. It's Zole again.

Zole's rubbing her hand around my waist. Felix is standing behind her staring at my eyes with a complex look on his face. There is a small yellow diamond-shaped pin attached to Felix's shirt. I can somehow read the tiny black letters on the pin. "Handling. Comfort. Quality. Value." I would say that my head is spinning, but that would sound stupid, right?

"How have you been?" asks Zole. "No, what I really want to ask you is *where* have you been. We've been looking all around here for you."

I open my mouth and for several seconds nothing comes out. Eventually the four words bashfully emerge from the dark hole. "Up in a tree."

"Up in a tree?" Zole looks massively entertained by the idea. But she knows more about me than her silly grin tells. "Have you found another favorite tree? You do know that your old tree was cut down?"

I feebly respond, "Yes."

See! She even knows about the saw. The saw. I can see the saw in the man's hands. I am barely able to ask her, "You knew about my tree?"

"Everyone who lives around here or just comes here

to relax knew about your tree."

"I was that obvious?"

Zole does a double double grin. "It's a small world."

-10-

SELF-EVIDENCE

I have found evidence that I am not alone in here.
Probably this space is a room, but it's so dark a room that I
am far from certain which way is up and which way down. I
can, however, hear someone's body breathing. Yes, my
body is breathing, too; I can hear *two* bodies breathing.
Which suddenly makes me remember what I said to you just
before I turned around however long ago and discovered
that Zole was behind me: "A more likely explanation, I
suppose, is that this area's time is cracking open. Does that
mean that there is another me somewhere around here
asking the same question?" Which makes me ask now in the
dark, is there another me somewhere around here
breathing? If there is not another me in here, then is that
the sound of my own breathing echoing off a wall or
something? Let me listen a moment. No, that other
breathing is working at a different pace than mine. And it's
more delicate. Then again, the properties of sound would
surely change (deform) if time were to suffer a severe
fracture. So, am I back to where I started with no evidence
at all that I have company in this blackness?

That's what we need—light! A golden glow fills the
room. It *is* a room, a large windowless room with a bright
floor and its four walls lined with... What are they? They
look like old books in blonde wood cases, but I'm not sure.
The only blotches on the glowing floor are one bed with me
in it and, over in the other half of the room, another bed
with someone else in it.

I decide that I will jump up out of this absolutely clean bed and jaunt my Jolty Jone over there to that other bed and flick the person lying there on the nose, which wakes up most people. (Obviously I'm assuming that the person is alive and maybe sleeping and that the breathing sounds that are not mine are not a soundtrack.) But before I can figure out how to get the kivers off me, the wondrous light suddenly goes out. Then, just as suddenly, it is back on again. Brief as it was, that on-off-on is enough to change my mind about jumping out of bed. I climb out of the immaculate bed slowly and carefully so that I won't get caught in the middle of a heroic leap by the light going off on me again.

The floor is deliciously toasty under my feet. It feels like sun-warmed glass. I cannot see if the smooth, seamless floor is reflecting light or transmitting light. Could the floor be the sole source of the room's golden glow?

"Not only can she remember everything there ever was to remember, she…" The person on the other bed pauses talking and rolls his/her head to the side to look at me. "…she was here before either of us." For now, I will relate to this smallish person as a woman.

I had come to an abrupt halt in the middle of the floor the second that the woman started her soft, clear speaking. I took a couple more steps toward her while she was staring at me with her round brown eyes. I further approach her. About five feet from her bed, I stop to cradle my chin comically between the palms of my hands. "Where," I ask in my gentlest voice, "is here?"

Smallish is right. An adult but very tiny. Her shoulders are not much over half as wide as mine. Her head is as round as her eyes and bears a frizzy crop of black hair. Her skin—the skin on her face is a grey-blue-brown with a rough texture that reminds me of nothing as much as a gunnysack, better known perhaps as a burlap bag. Then I realize that the color and texture of her facial skin are an illusion. I can see the illusion shifting. Is this mirage being produced by the strange light in the room? And the woman is not as small as she at first seemed. Actually, she is growing larger right before my eyes. I futilely call out to Taxi—who *aged* right before my eyes—and wake up.

"Good morning."

I awoke on a many-color bed in a sunny room, and Zole is standing at the foot of the bed greeting me.

"How'd you sleep?"

"Fine, fine," is what I answer. And that's not a lie. I did sleep well. One less-than-pleasant dream is not enough to make me badmouth an entire night. If it was an entire night. I don't remember going to bed in this room. But here I am.

Does Zole know my name? I ask her that.

"Of course I know your name, Jolty Jone. So does Felix. I've known your name all my life long."

I'm sitting up on the lovely bed, but I have to lie back down flat on my back a moment to consider that news.

+

Who was the woman standing under the tree?

I am pushed gently toward an open shower stall. I step into the stall and look around. It sort of feels the way being in a casket might feel but pleasantly so. I examine the handles, the sprayer. *I do, I do.* I do remember how to work a contraption like this. (I must have forgotten to close the shower door, though. Someone closes it for me. I was probably spraying water all over the bathroom floor.) When finally I'd had enough hot water sprinkled on me from my head to my toes, I remember something else: how to turn off the handles without burning myself. I have a bit of difficulty opening the door, yet I manage. And when I step out onto a fluffy white mat, I know that the next thing I am supposed to do is dry myself off. I spot a towel hanging on a silver bar attached to the wall right beside me. I grow suspicious and check the label on the terry cloth towel. It does not say MAIDEN'S WORK in red letters. It says MADE BY SAFE BOX in green letters. What do towels have to do with boxes, safe or not? Perhaps that is not to be known.

I had just finished drying myself when Felix saunters into the room with a stack of clothes between his hands. He winks at me, sits the stack on the counter, and leaves without a word.

Sure they fit. Sure they are beautiful. There is a question, however: do I want to wear these clothes out of this room? Several facts (ha-ha) say yes. I've got a name now/again; I spent the night in a regulation bed; I've had an inside shower first thing in the morning. Several facts (ha-ha) say no. I have no idea what is going on or how I got here; I am comfortable living outside; I could easily dump my name again.

"We burned your other clothes, Jolty," says Zole on her way by the open bathroom door, "just in case you were thinking you don't want to wear those clothes you have on."

She is a mindreader, that Zole. So I guess I'm stuck with these threads for the time being. I straighten the clothes on my body.

I smell food cooking. Someone calls my name. I follow the sound to a kitchen. This room feels familiar. But it's my experience that heating and stirring garlic and onions and other fresh stuff in a pan always puts out a smell that makes me think I know this place.

I look past smiling Zole and smiling Felix and out the window, because I hear words coming in the window, harsh words. "Stick your finger up your squat, you blah blaa-blaa!"

This is a new voice. I step quickly over to the window and look out. *No one.* A lush, well-maintained vegetable garden surrounded by flowers is all that I see.

"What is it, Jolty?"

I turn to Felix. "I heard someone out there speaking as if they were talking to someone in this room."

"Do you know who it was?"

"No, Felix."

He smiles when I call him by name.

"I didn't hear anyone," says Zole.

"Neither did I" says Felix.

"But I did," says me.

Felix and Zole shrug at me, both of them at the same time. Then, silently, they return to what they were doing.

So I look around the kitchen, at the ceiling and the floor, at the sink and the counters, at the cabinets and appliances, at the table and chairs.

"You can sit anywhere you like, Jolty. Just pick a chair and sit down. The food's all but ready."

Yahh. I will take Zole up on her offer. Choosing the chair closest to the hall door and lowering my butt to its padded seat, I have an ok view of the window that the voice had come in.

"Food!" barks Felix as he drops a steaming plate of chow on the table mat in front of me. "Eat it up!"

Felix zips back to the counter to the right of the stove and returns to the table with another big plate. He drops that plate on the next place mat around the table to my right. "Food, Zole!" Felix is grinning broadly while he's shouting orders. "Eat it up!"

Zole shakes her head in amused disapproval. She takes off her color-splashed apron—that matches Felix's—and sits down where she was told to, just as Felix is returning to the table with a third plate. He sits down on my left facing Zole.

I am thinking that I am just about to let go of my name and disappear into a tree again, when Zole lays her hand over mine on the table. "It's so good to have you in the house again."

Felix immediately chimes in. "It sure is!"

Quickly he adds, "Eat it up!"

We ate it up. And licked our plates clean. Then we all three vanished in the storm that came down upon us from the north.

+

Talky talky talky! Walky walky walky! Mocky mocky mocky! Turn around! Look out! Do down! Do up!

"Tell me a story, Jolty."

"Your story is not mine, Zole. My story is not yours. There is no way to hear someone else's story."

"Are you completely convinced of that?"

"I am."

"If people cannot hear each other's stories, Jolty, why do they think that they love each other?"

"If you turn that last question of yours into a statement, you will have a good beginning for a definition of *love*, Zole."

"Turn my question into a statement?"

"Exactly."

"How?"

"For example—just for example: 'People cannot hear each other's stories, so they think that they love each other.'"

"Not many people are going to want to view their relationships that way."

"Or you might try this, Zole: 'People who love each other think they cannot hear each other's stories.'"

"That's not much better."

"Or this one: 'People who think they *can* hear each other's stories—"

"Enough, Jolty. Enough. I get your point that it's all just a bunch of words, and you can put them in any order you want, even if you end up with a meaningless sentence."

"Yes, and Love stays."

Zole smiles sweetly and hugs her cheek against my shoulder. "And Love abides."

Zole and I are sitting side by side on her living room floor, leaning back with our elbows raised to rest them on the seat of the couch behind us. I don't know where Felix is until he walks by close in front of us and says/proclaims without looking down at either of us, "A new recognition of the vagaries of life." Not ten seconds later, he walks by us again, going in the opposite direction. As he passes he mumbles, "Spacious syntax." And our man is again trekking his by now well-worn path in front of us when he stops and turns to say clearly and directly to both of us, "Huyuhyuh?"

Who am I to be talking about Love with a capital *L*? The subject has forever escaped me, forever now and forever before now and forever after now. —Yuck! Why did I say *that*? Just to hear my mind moving as my head falls to the side? I surrender to sleep, a warm sleep indoors in the daytime with a belly full. And I'm not alone.

Now ain't that a grunch of slap! All things considered, sitting here on the floor with Zole I must have sounded like I had self-anointed myself as The Infallible Guide, the deliverer of enigmatic revelations that will forever change the lives of those who hear them. No wonder Felix started acting like a walking, talking oracle himself. He was trying to show me how I sounded. Therefore, I will curl my body up in a smaller and smaller ball until no one can account for my whereabouts. And in a ball that small there is no room for a name, not even a short two-word name like Jolty Jone.

-11-
REBUILDING

That *was indeed* an offbeat trip! Remind me to never repeat it.

And...? Wasn't there something else you were supposed to remind me of? Oh, yeah. Ridding my life of its *if*'s and *maybe*'s. Think, think, having thought about it, no, I'm not ready today to eject those two invaluable words. So you don't need to remind me about that. In fact, you might as well just forget all about reminding me about that.

"So where are you?"

Aghh! Another voice behind me. I shant turn around. I shant do anything but ignore. Ignore! Ignore! Ignore! (Yes, I'm aware that to ignore something means I make myself ignorant of it. A little well-placed ignorance prevents stomach ulcers, you know.)

But when a hand lays itself on my shoulder, I do turn around, quickly.

"Haven't seen you for a while. So where are you? What are you doing? Where've you been? Etc."

Who is this person talking to me?

"You don't recognize me? No, I can see that you don't. And for good reason: it's been a long long time."

"It must have been." My hollow reply has a definite snottiness to it. Why?

"Mob B'hoy. That's me, the roughneck Mob."

I nod my head. The name fits him. He looks like he would pop me in the teeth if given just half a chance. (See! That *if* works there.) Even so, he is dressed very nicely, as nicely as an elegant lady might dress. Nice colors, nice cut to his clothes, sharply pointed shoes.

"What are you doing out here all by yourself on this fine sunny day?" he genteelly inquires. "Just taking a walk through the trees?"

"Yes." Am I lying to him? No. Although I have no where in mind to go after this walk, I *am* just taking a walk through the trees.

I am almost convinced that this man is merely a stranger trying to pick me up when he calls me by the name I had just, barely managed to forget.

"Jolty, Jolty Jone, oh where have you been, my sweet Jolty Jone?"

His sweet Jolty Jone? Duh! I think it's about time I flee the scene.

Suddenly he says, "Zink!"

"Zinc?"

"That is right. Zink!"

Evidently he's trying to give me a clue of some kind. But *zinc* does nothing in my head but make me think of the bluish-white metallic element of that name. Is that what he is talking about? I shrug my shoulders at him.

He explains. "The *z* is for sleep, like 'catching up on my z's.' And the *-ink* is for *think*. Don't you remember, Jolty? *Thinking while you're asleep!* We used to have contests, you and I, to see who could come up with the far-outest thought while we were asleep."

It's the friendly talk that's making his mean-looking face impress me so oddly. His face is not exactly grotesque looking. It's not quite an overdone handsome either. Maybe *distorted* is the word I'm searching for. (See! I think the *maybe* worked, too.) Is it distorted by the show of friendliness, or is his face permanently that way?

I have to ask. "How old are you thinking we were when we supposedly had these *contests*?"

"Supposedly? You don't believe me! You're thinking I'm some kind of weirdo come alongside to attack you."

His face is not permanently the way it was, because it has changed. His face has moved closer to the grotesque. I shift uneasily on my feet. "I don't know what to think right at this moment."

"And how do you suppose I know your name, Jolty?"

"I am constantly surprised by how many people know my name."

Mob B'hoy steps closer. He sets his big hand against the side of my neck. "We were five when we started the contests, somewhere around eight when we stopped them."

Am I remembering this guy, or is he planting his story in my head? "Why did we stop them?"

+

I am seeing this person. I am constructing this person from pieces and parts, from fleet glimpses, from shards of my experiences, my experiences from before time, from before this time. My ever enlarging memory. My everblooming memory. If I open my eyes now, the man will be either standing there in front of me completely familiar to me or he will be gone, erased.

I open my eyes to look up at the sky. A cloud, having appeared from out of nowhere, is moving across the sun. The day goes from bright and sunny to dread grey in three bats of my eyelids. I lower my eyes to where Mob B'hoy's face would have been if he had been there. My professed childhood friend has vanished.

"We stopped them because…"

Aghh! Another voice behind me. I shant turn around. Then I realize it is Mob B'hoy's voice. Someone slaps me on the shoulder. Must be Mob.

"I fooled you, Jolty. I ducked around back of you while your eyes were closed."

"What are you doing back there now?"

"Admiring your backside, Jolty. You're not eight years old any more, you know."

Hence, I do turn around.

He looks pretty much the same. He's smiling again. His features seem a bit better fixed on his face although he is not yet perfectly clear. I would still categorize his face as mean-looking. How would he categorize my face?

"Not bad, Jolty."

"What?"

"You asked how I would categorize your face, and I answered with underspoken praise."

"*Underspoken* is a word?" (His *not bad* used as positive praise is an example of litotes, not of so-called *underspeaking.*)

"I just used it, didn't I. Stands to reason then that *underspoken* must be a word."

If I'm making this person up as I go, I can see why he isn't coming into focus: I don't like him. What can I do to be rid of what I have made of him so far? Yes, I wish he would disappear completely and permanently. Then he wouldn't be answering questions I haven't asked out loud. Maybe I could climb up in a tree and die again. That sounds like fun. Let me look around for a suitable tree.

+

You probably guessed it. Yes, it took me a while but I found the *same* tree. I climbed up in it, went to sleep, woke up again, and saw that same woman on the ground below me, as if no time at all has passed since the first time I climbed this tree (to die). So I repeat my line from that first time, out loud this time: "Who do I spy standing below me with arms spread pleadingly and her head laid back so that she can fully gaze up at me?"

"I am your fondest admirer. I hang on your every available word."

She did not sound sincere. She sounded like she was taunting me.

I ask her, "Do you have a name?" Waxing sardonic, I add, "Or should I address you as My Only and One and Therefore Fondest Admirer?"

"Sure I have a name. If you come down here, we can talk about it."

"You won't bite me?"

"I do not bite anyone." Waxing ironic, she adds, "Ever."

"Ok, I'm on my way down."

I never move too fast, not up, down, or across the face of the planet. I have discovered that each place in this world is a unique space, and I have watched others speeding around so fast that the spaces they pass through don't have time to get established in their brains. These people necessarily experience life as confusing. My excuse for taking so long to climb down out of the tree is that I am avoiding this confusion. I sing as I climb, "Putting in on the left, taking out on the right."

I stand with my hands hanging at my sides and my feet together on the grass at the base of the tree, awaiting whatever is to come.

"Why the big scowl, Jolty? You always did overplay your part. Try smiling at me. You might even give me a big hug. After all, we were once almost united in illusion."

"What illusion?"

"I stand corrected. *You* never thought of what you were doing as manufacturing illusion. You actually believed you were visiting vast golden vistas and taking me and others with you on the power of your words and thoughts."

In a strong-willed, overly intelligent kind of way, the woman is *a looker*. I remind her. "You promised me your name if I came down to you."

"I did. I did."

She twirls her vertical index finger. I don't know what that is supposed to mean. She floats the finger high in the air and then turns it into a pointer that she pushes against my chest. "Why can't you remember my name, Jolty?" Her eyes are flashing.

"Because I don't remember you."

"How could you *not* remember me?"

"Because I have never seen you before. For all I know, you are an actress using me for practice."

Her eyes narrow, and now *she* scowls. "That is absurd. And even if it were not absurd, if I were an actress out looking for someone to practice on, I could have used somebody already on the ground."

"Yes. You could have. But getting me to come down from the tree could have been the type of challenge you felt you needed today."

"You are looking right at me, Jolty. You truly don't remember me?" She softens her face, I assume to aid me in recognizing her.

"I do not."

Suddenly the woman lifts her blouse to show me a long scar below her right breast. "Remember that?"

"Yes." I have no idea why I said yes or why I then say, "*That* I remember."

"And do you remember my name now?"

"No."

"It's Rei Reus."

I simply shake my head no.

Exasperated but not yet angry, the woman shakes her own head no. Quietly she says, "I remember you talking to us, Jolty Jone. You spoke so openly, so expansively that it was as if you had no self and you had no idea that anyone else was burdened with the concept of self. But then, on the other hand, I remember you saying, once upon a time, 'No one delivers in the long run. That's why you have to get out early.' Is that why you were up there in a tree? You wanted out early but couldn't die?"

"Oh, I died recently."

"And you're back?"

Rei Reus? Doesn't strike any bells. "And I'm back."

"How was it?"

"It was as if I were living someone else's life. No,

more than one person's life. And I was still myself too."

"You were dead, Jolty, but you were aware of things—like in a dream?"

"Only sort of like a dream. Death didn't have any substance at all."

"Dreams have substance?"

"Dreams are far more substantial than this death thing was."

Now I remember the words. *Rei* is the plural of *reus*, and a reus is the defendant, the real person in a law case, as opposed to the *actor*, the plaintiff, the doer in the legal action. But does that matter? Does the history of the words mean anything here? Words like *rei* or *reus* or *star* or *court* or *miles* or *moon* or *silver* or *fisher* usually lose their worldly meaning when used as a person's name. It just occurred to me that Rei Reus is another two-word name. Yet...let me think. If the first name is the plural of the last, then don't we end up with more than two words?

"I'll have to take your word for that, Jolty. I've never died and known it." The woman rubs the side of her nose with that pointer finger of hers. "But let's back up, please. Jolty, why were you in that tree?"

"Rei." I'll address her as Rei—why not?—if that's what she wants. "Why were you down here on the ground looking up at me?"

"Why'd you call me Rei if you don't remember my name?"

"Because you just told me that your name is Rei Reus?"

A light comes on for her? "So you can remember my name for a couple of minutes at a time?"

I raise both of my pointer fingers and press one to either side of my nose. "I am not going to answer hostile questions."

"I didn't mean it as hostile."

"I think you did, dear."

"All right, Jolty, I'll try again. Can you remember the names of someone, anyone, who you talked to *yesterday*?"

I study that question for a long while. It smells like a trick question. Before I even begin to formulate an answer, RR says, as if to herself, "So you cannot remember yesterday." She raises her hand—probably to rub her nose again—but quickly drops the hand to her waist. "Have you talked to anyone besides me *today*?"

"No."

"Are you sure?"

"Yes, Rei." I kinda like saying her name. "It was quite dark when I mounted the tree and went to sleep. And you are the only person I have seen since I awoke. I am quite sure."

"Can you remember, right now, anyone's name besides yours and mine."

"Of course I can."

Rei is waiting for something. I don't know what she is waiting for. I've already answered her question.

She must have gotten tired of waiting, because she fans her hand back and forth three or four times as she turns her head away from me. She looks like she's going to walk.

"Don't go away, Rei."

She stops before she has taken a step, looks back at me, pauses, frowns, smirks slowly, and returns to me. "I won't leave you, Jolty."

Was it just me? Or did I hear her mind saying "…like you left me…"? Her lips were definitely not moving. Zingo! Is that the way I sounded to Mob B'hoy?

"Did you hear me, Jolty?"

What? Oh, she's just regular-talking now. I'll answer her, and maybe she will explain. "I heard you say something after you said that you wouldn't leave me."

"Did you hear me say '…like you left me…'?"

"That's what I heard all right." I think I'm shaking now. Or at least shivering. "Did you say it out loud?"

"No! Certainly not. I did not use my vocal cords whatsoever."

She cocks her head funny and stares at my eyes, as if she is realizing something significant. "You are the one who taught me how to do that, Jolty. Have you forgotten how to speak and hear that way? Like you had forgotten my name?"

"I don't think I know what you are talking about."

"Sure you know what I'm talking about, JJ. Try a little harder."

JJ and RR? Now that pair of twins sounds familiar. Hmm. Are they sounding familiar merely because I thought of her as RR just a short while before she called me by my own set of matching initials? No, I'm certain there is something else I should remember. JJ and RR. RR and JJ? Suddenly I'm on a sailboat way out on a deep blue sea. Ugh! This boat is merely a distraction; my brain wants to be let off the hook. What does it not want to remember?

My my. Napa noollie. What am I wanting to happen?

-12-
SUBTLE LAYERS

Rei, framing her face with her hands, watches me out the corner of her eyes. "You see yourself as a shade moving about the earth unnoticed by the vast majority of humans, don't you, Jolty?"

Is she asking or telling me? Sitting next to her on the grass, out in the open, away from the shelter of the trees, I hold my head audaciously aloof and ask out the corner of my mouth at the corners of her eyes, intentionally mis-mimicking with my hands what her hands are doing around her face, "Which answer, yes or no, would make what you already have planned to say easier to say?"

"A yes."

"Then I'll answer yes, Rei, just to make things nice for you."

Her watching wavers not. She dons her patent grin. "You understand, I hope, Jolty, that this is not how others see you."

"I have little idea how anyone sees me."

"They see you the same way you see them, each and all of you wrapped in your own literal, common, basically impotent world."

"Is that how I see people, Rei? I never knew that. I am truly amazed at your certainty."

She continues, vinegar sharp in her linguistry and not in the slightest bit intimidated by my sharp doubt and sarcasm. "These other persons—correct me if I'm wrong. Their actions, their words have forced you to assume that their (conscious) worlds do not include the subtle layers you see yourself (consciously) moving through. It seems to you that their (conscious) worlds are only *there*, that life has these people merely shuffling about, manipulating icons, dancing whichever dance comes along."

"Right or wrong, up or down, green or black."

"That sounds like *you* replying all right, Jolty. But at one time I would have thought it meant something."

"With that said, Rei, what would you have me do now? Fall back on the ground sobbing? Rise forever into the blissful sky? I could make a new start. I could make an old start. I could do something or nothing. I could go on forever like this and end up with nothing or something."

Rei grins again and tells me a short story. "Blacky smiled. He jumped up on his horse and rode. He rode way out into the wilderness. And when he returned, he had little or nothing to say about his trip. He was still smiling, however. He sold his horse to buy two pairs of fancy hiking boots."

My head nods its approval. "Good allegory." (Is that what is called an *allegory*? I get all the words of that kind mixed up.)

"You could see yourself in the story then?"

"Myself? I thought the story was about you, Rei."

Quickly she shakes her head in disapproval. "No, you didn't. You are just being tiresomely evasive."

"Evasive? Tiresome?" I roll my head on my shoulders, roll my head, roll my head, drop my chin to my chest. "Am I being attacked? The grand isolated hammer awaits my skull? I'll shortly be x-ed out? A yes-or-no answer will suffice." I can't help but snicker. "Hence is't, that I be betrayed by the mutinous crew." I don't know who that's a quote from, if anybody. I used the word *crew* because Rei keeps talking about "these other persons" as if there were once a group, that included her, hooked and hanging close to me somehow. Therefore I said *crew*.

The scar on her…her torso provoked some kind of response from me, but I do not recognize the woman. I do not! As far as I can tell, all this could be fantasy. *The real part* in each of "these other persons," including Rei, could have evaporated while I was asleep or dead, leaving behind only crusts, moving crusts with memories. The memories in each of these many crusts would be the memories that had belonged to whichever person the individual crust looks like, yet the crust would be without a soul. (Fear not for my mental state: I used the word *soul* hesitantly.) And so I wouldn't recognize them. Stop! What am I saying? That would mean—wouldn't it?—that this crew did at one time exist. It would also explain why RR recognizes me, and I don't her. Or is it actually not the crew that's missing but the *me*? That's a good thought. What could I do about that? I could strip the capital letters off my name: *jolty jone*. Then no one would know that it's a name and there'd be no further need for a me. That's *not* a good thought. Doesn't add up. In fact this whole last paragraph doesn't add up to piddle. — Back to Rei.

Let me sneak in another quick thought here, in the form of a question. My fantasizing about soulless crusts that I may or may not have once known as people—am I confusing myself into believing this woman Rei?

Whatever. I am returning now to Rei and her name-calling.

No! Lo, someone steps out of the mental haze and

into our idyllic setting. Rei and Jolty would have jumped a foot in the air in surprise had they not been sitting down. (Notice that I did not un-capitalize my name there. No use trying to hide out here in the open.)

Rei might have jumped only half of a foot. For she seems to know the strange new person. Jane Hupiter.

Jane Hupiter.

Jane Hupiter.

Five distinctly different expressions appear on Rei's face before she climbs to her feet and says, "It might surprise you, Jane, to hear me say that I'm glad you came."

The new arrival replies to Rei in an absolutely delicious voice that reminds me of milk and blowing leaves. "Are you having troubles with Jolty already, Rei?"

"No! Not that kind of trouble!" Rei sounded a touch defensive that time. She wiggles her hand at nothing. "Jolty didn't—and I think *doesn't*—recognize me."

The woman turns from Rei when I stand up. "Do you recognize me," she asks, looking me straight in the eyes.

I look back into her eyes. I see no self-doubt in there, none.

The woman is as familiar as my own thumb, but I have never before seen her. "I know that your name is Jane Hupiter, but I do not know you."

"Just that quick, you're ahead of me, Jane," exclaimed Rei. "I had to tell Jolty my name."

"Yes, my name is Jane Hupiter. You are Jolty Jone, am I right?"

"It would seem so."

Rei scratches her head feverishly with both her hands, and scratches it some more, thoroughly, vividly mussing up her hair. "As you just heard for yourself, Jane, Jolty is being even more evasive than normal."

With a comical cock of her head, Jane asks me, "Is that at all possible?"

I shoot back, "How would I know what constitutes a normal level of evasion for Rei?"

"I think you're right, Rei. JJ is being even more evasive than normal."

These two people want me to believe in them. They are using all kinds of tricks to get me to believe in them.

"We want you to believe in us, Jolty." Jane's eyes are those famous ancient pools an uncountable number of people have lost their way in. "We have both known you for quite a long time. I for a bit longer than Rei. And you have known us. You have known us for a long time."

My eyes grow wide in horror. "You are eternal beings!"

Jane shows me her beautiful smile. "No, we are humans like you, dippy."

She takes me by the arm. And Rei takes me by the arm.

Arm in arm the three of us are walking away. Walking away. To where? Walking. Walking. Time passes. It's a pleasant walk. And passes. Look over there! That's where my Hossmattcha-watching tree once stood. Gone away it is. Away away. Nothing left but the flowers.

"It's gone, Jolty."

"I know, Jane." How did she know what I was looking at? Or does everyone know everything about me? That's probably the truth right there. I'm the ugly goldfish in the tiny fishbowl atop the knee-high pedestal that everyone passes twice daily on their way back and forth across the town square. And they all call me JJ for short. JJ the goldfish.

I've not heard Jane talking to me like Rei did, without using her voice that is. Come to think of it, I have not noticed anything like that coming from Rei again. Maybe it doesn't work if there are more than two people present. Maybe the invisible wires get all crossed up. If I am the one who taught Rei how to speak and hear without speaking and hearing, who taught me? Must there always have been a teacher? No, that's why we have put together the word *self-taught*. Right?

And looking out farther, way beyond the x-ed tree, who do I see? Right again. Hossmattcha. She's standing at her bus stop, waiting for her bus. Can she see me? Would she recognize me if she did? Has she ever seen me?

"Yes, yes, and yes."

Ugh, ugh, and ugh! That was Jane with the three yes's. I heard them with my ears, but her ears are not how she heard my three unvoiced questions. Is she hearing me right now?

"No," says Jane.

"Great," say I. I say it loudly out loud.

Rei swings her head out in front of us to examine my face. We are still walking, of course. "Great what, Jolty?"

I get the funny feeling these two women are teaming up on me, maybe even making fun of me. Optimism! Remembering this questionable philosophical doctrine, I decide that I will consider Rei and Jane's intentions to be all in good fun. Or are they working some kind of therapy on me? Or are they working another trick on me to get me to believe in them? Do they desperately need me to trust them for some unknown-to-me reason? It does feel nice to have them one on either side of me. Three we's in a wod.

So the dream is over. I was sure it had all been a dream.

Yet when I look to my left at Rei, she winks at me. When I glance to my right, Jane winks at me. We are still walking, of course.

+

We have been walking for years. Seasons approach, seasons pass. Babies are born, pompous old codgers die. I'm starting to sweat.

We walk for about an hour and stop before a door in a concrete wall. Jane takes a key out of her pocket, puts the key into a lock on the door, turns the key, and pushes the door open.

So the dream is over. I was sure it had all been a dream.

Wrong again. We three step into the building. Jane closes and locks the door behind us. It's dark in the room, but it's not so dark that I can't make out the alien life-forms lining the walls.

Rei is doing something that I can't see. Turns out she was opening the heavy drapes that covered a giant square window. Lots of light pours into the space. The alien life-forms are three-dimensional sound absorbers. That's why it's so quiet in here. Even with the drapes open now, I can just barely hear the noises of the city. I am even eerily aware of the nearly silent sound of the air coming in through registers on the floor. There is nothing else in the large room, no furniture, nothing.

Jane motions to me. "Follow me."

She leads me to an open staircase, and we climb the stairs to the room above. One room on each floor. No third floor.

The room on the second floor is furnished. Living room, bedroom, kitchen, bath and sink and flush toilet—all in the one large room. There's no ceiling. I can look up through the exposed rafters at the roof and see a clear skylight above the bed. I instantly find the room comfortable. It's familiar too.

I step over and look out a broad, tall, wood-cased window at the greenery across the street. Below the window is a bus stop. I turn back around to see what Jane and Rei are doing.

This is Jane's room, I think. Yet Rei was familiar enough with the room downstairs to open the drapes in the dark.

+

A notion is forming...

Hah! You already surmised that the room was mine. Didn't you? Well Jane is about to say the same thing, that the room was once mine.

"This building is yours, Jolty."

Yikes! That's what Jane said: the building *is* mine. Rei nods affirmatively.

That would be nice if it were true. That's nice even if it isn't true. I like this room. And the spooky space downstairs, too.

If it's mine, why don't I just take off my clothes and

lie down on that bed? It would feel good to stretch out there in the hatched rectangle of sunlight. Beats me why not. But I don't. I look at Jane, at Rei. They are waiting for me to say something, I know. I press my hands to my cheeks in pretense of innocence.

+

I'm not alone. I'm on a bed. There's a person on either side of me. They are both asleep or doing an excellent job of sounding like it. They're mostly covered with a sheet and blanket, yet I'm sure they are Jane and Rei.

It's *my* bed. It's morning, and the sun is shining in the window that looks out over *the* bus stop. I can't see all six windows of the room from where I'm lying, but I remember them from last night. There are two on the east wall, two on the west wall, and one window each on the north and south walls. I can see the other east window too. It's in the kitchen area. The sun is shining in through it too.

If I exhale? That is the question. I have taken in a deep, *belly*-filling breath. It's there, inside me, showing no sign whatsoever that it intends to ever come out. If I pay no attention to it, maybe the breath will just sneak out by itself.

Rei has dark reddish hair. Jane has brown-to-black hair. And I—we've discussed this before. Every hair of mine, anywhere on me, is the whitest white.

It worked. Somewhere in there I exhaled.

Should I lie here until they wake up? Or should I get up and make myself at home? Or should I slip clear out of here forthwith?

"Morning, Jolty."

"Morning, Rei."

"Morning, Jolty."

"Morning, Jane."

That takes care of that.

Rei's scar. The bitterness in her voice sometimes. The powers of the distorted, conceptual mind.

We bathe, all three of us at once, in the tub-shower. The two of them then towel me off, and Jane leads me to a beautiful old hand-carved wardrobe standing proudly against the wall. Do I recognize any of the clothes in this freestanding closet? You bet I do not.

The clothes all appear to be handmade. Jane tells me, "These are your clothes, Jolty." They fit my body very nicely. I accept them, temporarily.

Now that I am dressed, I'm going to stand right here where I am and wait for Rei and Jane to get dressed. They can't just walk around the room naked all morning drying their hair. If this is *my* building, they won't have any fresh clothes to put on. Right? But, actually, they *could* just prance around all morning "naked as jay birds," though I don't myself consider birds as naked. Birds are more like *permanently clothed.*

Or I could go over and look out the window. Would I see Hossmattcha stepping off the bus? I realize I could be making all this up, yet I'm assuming from Jane's three yes's yesterday morning that the stop below this window is the other end of Hossmattcha's bus ride, the *other* other end being across the street from my x-ed tree. Where would Hossmattcha be going every morning if she does get off the bus outside?

"She's coming up here, Jolty. Her bus will be arriving in five or so minutes."

Yuk! How am I going to have any privacy at all if Rei and Jane, Rei in this case, are all the time doing that *hearing me thinking* thing? Ahh! Yes! The answer is quite obvious. I can stop their eavesdropping altogether with just a sliver of change in the position from which I talk inside. I've been talking in here as if I am orating to the outside. So from now on I will only talk confidentially to you or confidentially to the mirror in my head. No more broadcast thinking around these two women. And not around Hossmattcha too, if she actually does show up here.

Jane and Rei are smiling at me. They have both sat down on the edge of the bed. Are they smiling because they can still hear me thinking or smiling because they realize I have cut them off?

I am getting no answer. Neither of them are saying to me, "Because you *tried* to cut us off." Indeed they have looked away from me as if their attentions have switched to other matters. They each pull a suitcase from under the bed, and they get dressed.

+

Hossmattcha does not show up in the next five minutes or ten or twenty or even forty minutes. Rei is upset by this. Jane, however, says she figured last night that since Hossmattcha didn't come here yesterday after she saw me walking with Jane and Rei, Hossmattcha would not be coming here anymore. "Hossmattcha is a housecleaner who was hired to take care of the inside of the building while you were out, Jolty. And now you are back."

I myself am kinda glad Hossmattcha didn't walk in the door. I would not know what to say to her. Unlike Rei and Jane, Hoss I remember. Not as a housecleaner but as a bus patron. A friend almost. A distant friend.

+

For an hour and a half now a question has been presenting itself to my mind: Why didn't Rei and Jane just lead me across the street yesterday to get on the bus and ride here, instead of the three of us walking here, whether Hossmattcha would have agreed to accompany us on the bus or not? There are many possible answers to that question, but none of them are packing any special weight for me. I'll list just the first three unpleasant possibilities I thought of. Jane and Rei may have never before spoken to Hossmattcha. Jane and Rei may have dark feelings about Hossmattcha. Or, coming from the other direction, Hoss may thoroughly disapprove of Jane and Rei. Hey! The explanation doesn't necessarily have to be unpleasant. It may be no more than that Jane and Rei enjoy walking in the fresh air more than they like using public transportation. Or they may think that because I am fond of sitting up in trees, I would not like riding on a bus. Or they may somehow know that Hossmattcha likes to ride alone on her bus.

Jane is over in the kitchen area cooking something. Rei has gone downstairs. And I am still standing where R&J helped me get dressed.

Here's one more question: How come Jane called the woman who I used to see at a bus stop by the same name that I called her by, a name I have never said out loud to any living, breathing human?

WHILE STILL IN THE AIR

The jar.

The joy jar.

The joy jar rolls.

The joy jar rolls away.

This is not about what is going on here but about how to get out of here. My first attempt of the morning was to say the word *Loy* over and over to myself. That didn't work. (It has before.) My second attempt was the *jar* thing above. I only said the first four of the forty-four known lines before I gave up and decided to describe to you what I was doing. And that's where I am now.

A sign outside the north window names the street running along that side of the building as Pine Street. I picture a pothole many blocks away at the very end of Pine Street. A deep pothole that flamingos bathe in after a rainstorm. Or hippos. Or elephants. Or grizzly bears. All of these creatures are dead and gone, I know. But I remember seeing pictures of them. I actually saw a live wild bear once. I must have been a *child*. That's a strange word, *child*. A strange concept altogether.

It's nearly noon, I think. I carefully walk over to the bed and lie down. Look up at the skylight! There's a bird up there peering down through the glass and wire at me. Probably not. The bird is probably just admiring its own reflection on the outside of the glass. But that bird could easily perch up there at night and watch what is going on down in here. Maybe if I borrowed a powerful flashlight, I could suddenly turn it on in the nighttime and catch the bird studying me. Or maybe there would be a whole bunch of birds up there. I would wave to them, and then we'd all be friends.

Jane and Rei left—Rei yesterday evening and Jane this morning—to give me "some time alone with your things, Jolty." I think they were referring to the furniture and stuff. I have not opened any drawers or cabinets or such; so I don't know what else they could be talking about.

All is here?

Up! I get up from the bed and swagger over to the kitchen in search of food. On the table! On the table is a lone key. The key is the same color and the same basic shape as that one Jane used to open the door downstairs. Can I take it then, Sam, that I am free to come and go as I wish?

I gobble up some food and go, down and out, locking the door behind me. That's quite an experience: locking the door behind you. I step around the corner to the bus stop and stand there beside the sign pole until I see a bus coming, at which time I vamoose. Up the sidewalk, across the street, around the block, over the hump, etc.

That *was indeed* an offbeat trip! My own building! Imagine that!

"Over the hump"? Isn't that some kind of cliché? (I'm walking casually now.) But isn't everything a cliché? "Down and out…step around the corner…across the street…" People themselves may be clichés. Animals are *treated* like clichés. Trees? Trees are difficult to talk about in that vein.

I keep thinking there is someone behind me who is

going to speak out to me any moment now. Who would it be? Mack March. Yes, if I turned my head around to look, Mack March would be there behind me. But if I didn't turn my head to look? Who would it be? Probably reddish Rei. Or the bus driver wanting to know why I didn't get on the bus. Or another one of those someones whom I don't know but who think they know me.

Do I look back or don't I? I don't. I just walk, eyes forward, head held high, arms swinging gracefully at my sides. Then I hear a song weaving through the trees. (I'm back in the trees again.) I start weaving the same way through the trees, drifting down the music.

Nope. I have been going *upstream*. I come upon the singer. He is standing all alone in a circle of trees, singing upward as if he is serenading one of the trees. Or serenading someone up in one of the trees.

I approach him and walk all the way around him three times. He does not even notice me. (I'm confident of that, but I could be wrong.)

He stops singing and merely stands there. I walk up close in front of him. He looks at me as if for the first time. His mouth opens. His eyes open wide.

"Jolty Jone!"

Yep, this one's another one of those someones whom I don't know but who know my name. I did enjoy the way he said my name, though. He made it sound like a poem.

"I heard you had been retrieved!"

What did he mean by that? Am I a stick that a dog retrieves? I raise my hand to the level of my heart, then move it away from me horizontally and then down a bit to his heart. He jumps in obvious fright when my hand touches his shirt. He's shaking all over.

"How did you know my name."

"I have seen many pictures of Jolty Jone. All of us have."

"'Who is 'all of us'?'"

He knocks my hand away from his heart, turns like a rabbit and darts away. *Dart* is the wrong word: he *runs* away. He doesn't look back. He just keeps on running.

Shouldn't I be scratching my head as thoroughly as Rei did that time. *All of us have seen many pictures of Jolty Jone.* In there? Is there a clue in there? Is there in there a clue to something I would like to know? I shiver and dart (*dart* is a good word this time) a look over my shoulder. No Mack March. No Rei Reus.

+

Jane is the one who comes after me. Look back there. That's her. Wearing an orange one-piece suit and white shoes, she's not glancing left or right; she's just striding up the path. Seems Jane knows exactly where to find me.

She comes to a stop to stand stiff-kneed with her feet apart. She raises her hands to her hips. She's checking out my face when suddenly she smiles, like the heavens have just opened wide.

I smile back at her.

"You don't need to spend your nights outside anymore, Jolty."

I repeat the word of hers that I'm having the most

trouble with. "Need?"

Her smile dissolves. She looks hurt. "You don't like the building any longer?" she asks me almost sadly.

"I like the building just fine, Jane."

"So why weren't you there sleeping beside me last night?"

"I had things to do, places to be."

She is watching, watching, watching my face. I don't seriously think I am supposed to feel intimidated by her gaze; but what else could she be expecting of me? She is very nice to look at; so I watch her face right back.

She rushes to my side, takes my hand, and presses the whole side of her body against my side (she's facing in the same direction as me).

We stand like that for awhile.

"Will you come back with me now, Jolty?"

"Come back to where, Jane?"

"To your building."

"Sure. Why not."

+

She doesn't let go of my hand all the way back. We are a block yet from the building when I notice a bus waiting at the stop. As we get closer, I see there is no one on the bus, not even a driver. But the bus's engine is running. I glance up at the second story window above the bus. Rei is standing just inside the window watching our approach.

"Do you still have your key, Jolty. If you do, why don't *you* open the door."

I retrieve the key from my pocket and insert it into the heavy, solid door. As I push the door open, I notice it is maybe twice as thick as I thought doors usually are. I return the key to my pocket, and Jane and I step into the big, empty room. The drapes on the humongous square window are already open. In fact the drapes on an exactly matching window directly across the room are open, too. Lots of light streams in from opposite directions! Hmm. That new window looks right out at the bus.

"Hi!" Rei greets us from the staircase. I'm glad she's not all wrapped up in an orange one-piece suit, too. And no white shoes too. It appears from halfway across the room that she's crying. Tears, you know.

Jane had finally let go of my hand when I needed to use that hand to get the door key out of my pocket. This time she takes me by my elbow. She leads me to the stairs. What is it that I'm feeling? Subtle green waves of animosity passing between Jane and Rei?

We climb the stairs all in a pretty row: Rei, Jolty, Jane, step, step, step. As my head rises above the second floor, I see, looking right at me, a very large someone in a bus driver's uniform. He or she is sitting at the kitchen table, leaning forward with his or her thick forearms crossed on the tabletop. He or she does not even blink.

"Jolty and Jane, this is Joe Beemer, the driver of the bus outside." Rei is not whispering. She is speaking in a strong, clear voice. "He has been so kind as to come up here to relay a message from Hossmattcha *to her employer.*"

The bus driver gets up from the table (it's a man) and walks directly toward me, his eyes not leaving my eyes for one second. Were Rei's tears for me, or were they a result of what this man said to her in his dark, cavernous voice?

"Ms Reeves asked me to tell you…"

He apparently lost track of what he was trying to say. I suddenly realize that the man is not threatening me, as was my first hasty take; he is, in fact, conspicuously nervous. He's also missing his four upper-front teeth.

"She wants me to say to you that she liked coming here and tidying up your place every day. Now as you are back, she won't be coming anymore." He is staring into my eyes, I'm staring into his eyes—nothing is exchanged. "She wishes you would send the rest of her pay to her address that you have."

Fidgeting. That's what I'm doing. Nothing else. Just standing here not moving my feet or eyes but fidgeting with the entire rest of my body. Oh yeah, I'm fidgeting mentally too. How? Again and again I am weighing my continued—though incomplete and often inaccurate—usage of the word *whom*.

"Her address is in the desk drawer, Jolty." Jane takes me by my elbow again. "I'll help you send her her pay."

Joe Beemer's eyes jump like a mechanical switch to Jane's eyes. She says to him, "Thank you. Mr. Beemer. We will take care of Ms Reeves today."

Dismissed, Joe Beemer returns to the table for his hat and leaves the room without saying another word. His exit takes a while, however; for he walks like a big snowman.

No one of us speaks either. Then we hear the door slam downstairs. Rei quick-steps over to the window and waits for Joe Beemer to come around the corner and climb into his bus. He apparently does, and the bus roars away.

Rei rotates her body to face me. The tears immediately reappear in her eyes. She marches noisily over the floor to me. Her lips float up real close to my mouth, then glide breathtakingly near to my cheek, then hover right next to my ear. *Now* she whispers. "Please don't leave me again, Jolty."

Stepping back two steps, she waits for me to reply.

Rei will have to wait a long time.

Jane intervenes. "Are you hungry, Jolty?"

My eyes are now fixed on Jane's orange garment. I think I am about to faint.

Faint from hunger? No. From being cooped up inside the building? Probably not. I have not been inside that long yet. More likely I am thinking I am no longer a human. I feel more like a blanket. And a blanket would not be standing up like I am. A blanket would drop to the floor.

+

It's dark. Carefully I raise my head. It's true. I'm in *my* bed again, lying between Jane and Rei. I look up. It's true. The bird is up there looking down at me. Illuminated by the moon and/or the city's lights, the bird's brown-black feathers appear dirty white. The eyes, one at a time of course, flash bright yellow-green at me. I stare up at the skylight until I am quite convinced there is not a bunch more birds up there. One bird I can handle (forget about).

There are six windows on this floor. (I think I already said that.) Looking out the five windows visible from here on the bed, all that I see is the night's sky. No buildings, trees, hills, or hovering aircraft. Or hovering people. Or hovering dogs. Or buses. Wait! What's that I see? Is it indeed a hovering bus? No! It's the moon.

Well here's a puzzle. It's a full moon, and I'm not rising above the bed. When I sleep/slept on the ground, I always am/was pulled toward the moon when it gets/got full. Maybe there is something embedded in the walls and roof of this building that short-circuits all above-the-supporting-surface experiences. Or maybe the full moon talks to the ground and the ground agrees to let me fall up for a while; but the moon can't talk to this bed, which is already a story above the ground.

Suddenly there's a hand on me! The back of someone's hand is now lying peacefully on my stomach. Both of my bed partners—I just about said *bedpans!*—still sound as if they are sound asleep.

What if I had said *bedpans?* Would I have been commenting meanly on the women on either side of me? That doesn't sound like me. No. I think I nearly substituted *bedpans* for *bed partners* because I experienced a quick need to use a one-worder and *bedpans* was as close to *bed partners* as I could get on the fly and still be using just one word. No insult intended, I'm sure.

Ah! The hand just withdrew from my stomach. I don't know whose hand it was. It wasn't mine! Both of mine are still at the ends of my arms, and my arms are pointed straight up at the bird. Who just flew away.

"Why have you got your arms up in the air, Jolty?"

I lower my arms and hands softly to the bed behind my head. "Well, Jane, I was being a scarebird, but I do believe my job is done now."

"Why aren't you guys sleeping?" gurgles Rei.

"Jolty was pretending to be a scarebird."

"Oh."

Rei is back asleep before she is completely done saying that word. Jane lays her hand back on my stomach. I do recognize the hand.

+

What kind of what is that? Who would care? Why guess? Why talk about a person immersed in a culture as if such a situation actually exists? Or has *ever* existed. If I get paint on my hands, I wash the paint off.

You'd better duck! Here comes another one of those zingers from nowhere: *The tighter a person is constructed, the higher the pitch of the voice.*

I don't think that's so. Do you? Naw, it couldn't be. It's probably just one of those pitches that sound like they ought to be true but aren't. It's like comparing canvas to crystal glassware.

Two-stepping (one-two three-four) over to the table, I snatch up a paper tag that was just about to fall/blow off the edge of the tabletop. (There's nothing written or printed on this 2x3 tag, yet gradually the paper-tag's purpose will come clear. The fine texture of the paper is forming small letters. And these pale letters are forming themselves into an old-fashioned math problem.) "From the present back to the beginning of time, if 'x' is the number of buses that have taken a breather at the stop below the window, but you have been watching the stop closely only for not very long this morning, how many buses have you seen being piloted by Joe Beemer?" That's an easy problem. None! No Joe Beemer.

Maybe Joe and Hossmattcha took the money and ran. Maybe Joe was Hossmattcha dressed up like a man. Maybe Hossmattcha has always been Joe dressed up like a woman.

Why am I trying to make a simple, common, everyday thingaboo about two people into something complex? Let it go. Leave it be. Simple is simple. Is is is.

Am I sure of that? Not on your life! Why would anything be simple if it could be complex? Attraction, you know. Things like to hook up to other things. Could an unhooked thing even be said to exist? Still, that does not necessarily mean that Joe Beemer is permanently hooked to Hossmattcha Reeves.

If I knew enough to call her Hossmattcha, why wasn't I aware of the *Reeves* as well? Ooops! I felt a slip in my position there. Where am I headed *now*? Oh, let it not be to the little white cage that I saw a big spotted dog stuffed into.

Stuffed into a nebulous relationship with two women who I don't know...

What did you say? I could take the money and run? Not hardly. Money is of no interest to me. And sport balls certainly aren't either. So what else does one run with?

Jane and Rei are waking up. They, the both of them, turn their bodies to lie on their backs, to yawn up at the ceiling with their eyes still closed. They swing one arm each across the space between them, where I am supposed to be. All four eyes pop open, and the two heads crank around to examine the empty space. I look away because I don't want to see what Jane and Rei do next.

Again, it's not a problem that can not be answered.

I'm looking down, watching the bus stop sign from the kitchen window. The sign has not returned my look.

"Jolty."

Rei turns on the shower. Jane steps into the tub. Rei joins her in the tub. Jane looks out at me. She extends her arm and curls a finger at me. Rei whistles at me and slaps her bare thighs. This time I am not even the stick a dog retrieves, I'm the dog. I get down on my hands and knees, pick up a clothes hanger between my teeth, and join the two in the shower.

"Good, Jolty. Good!"

+

"Surface readings vs spatial renditions?"

Midday. I'm reading a short note that someone—it would have to have been either Jane or Rei—has scribbled on that tag I saved from a bad fall this morning. (The tag was technically blank this morning, now it's not.) And the answer would be a yes, I think, if the quoted line is implying that I can read the surface anytime but I have to *continuously* make space. I'm ignoring the "vs," though; I can't translate that satisfactorily.

Made it through the shower and getting dressed.

Made it through the breakfast.

Made it through the sorrowful partings.

Now I'm home alone again.

The tag is lying more or less where I left it on the table before Jane and Rei woke up. (True, I read the question on the tag not a minute ago. But I did not touch or move the tag at all at that time.) Now, like it or not, I'm going to turn the tag over. And it's over. And it's blank. Technically speaking, the tag is blank on the second side.

Untechnically speaking? I'm no longer looking at the tag; so I don't know what it's gradually showing.

I'm looking out the window. I'm no longer looking out the window, I'm looking at the sink. I'm no longer looking at the sink, I'm looking at *looking at*.

Behind those two cloud-white words, I spot several brightly colored cartoon figures, moving...perhaps dancing. The words, the figures—illusions produced by pressures on the eyeballs, right?

So! What is their plan? Why did they leave me here by myself again? What do they expect me to do?

Reconsidering my plight, I realize I don't in any way know I am alone in the building. No, I'm only certain that I'm alone on *this floor* of the building. There could be a surprise party waiting for me downstairs.

Should I get dressed before I go down to check out the lower room? Why bother. I wander over to the top of the stairs and peer down into the room. Deep green water with white caps and sharks. It's the open sea down there! Looks like I'll be remaining up in this room awhile.

-14-
FOURTEEN FEET

The jar. The jar. The jar. Written in ten's. Twenty-three ten's. Twenty-three times ten. Written in seven's. And two's. Stand up! Turn around! Sit back down! Yah. Yah. Yah. OK. I'm tired of being in here. I'm sufficiently tired of being in here! I'm leaving, even if I have to swim across that room down there and then dive fourteen feet and hold my breath while I'm unlocking the door, all the while fighting off voracious fish and worrying about getting shot out the opening door like a cannonball. Hope a bus isn't going by right then.

The room on the ground floor is as dry and empty as it ever was. Both sets of shades are open. No unexpected problems arise as I descend the stairs and walk across the room. Having unlocked the door, I am reaching for the handle when I am taken by an admittedly silly idea that the ocean is now on the other side of the door. It's right outside there waiting for me, waiting for me to open the door so that it can roar-r-r back in here. But if *that* is a silly idea, in what category would I put the original, sudden-sea-in-a-room idea? Indecision. Yes, both of those ideas resulted from my indecision. But now I am out.

So what's for me to do out here? I check and, nope, there's no idling bus to peer around the corner at. That bench across Pine Street is empty. But do I really want to sit over there and stare at *my* building? Of course not. So what *would* I like to be staring at? Wow! Nothing comes to mind!

Except getting me a tune-up. But I shouldn't be

having that thought already. Didn't Jane and Rei do a thorough tune-up on me just last night? *Turn it off, Jolty!*

When I said, "nothing comes to mind," I was talking about a negative *nothing*, where no thing at all presents itself to the mind. I was not referring to any of the positive nothings, like "the void" or "the emptiness."

I close one eye and look out my other eye—*positive* and *negative* have switched positions. I cover both of my eyes and watch while +&- are switching back again. The switching process makes me think of the impossible. I assume it is not possible to have a flowing sheet of mercury, a sheet so very thin and supple it seems to be completely weightless, a sheet so very thin and supple that it could be the mind itself. If not the mind, then it's the membrane separating the mind from the everyday world. And if it's not that membrane—

Did I see them coming? Not me. Not until just now. I was too busy cerebrating.

Not a tricorn metaphor for snow capped peaks.

Not an arrow-headed team of white maned horses.

How could the approachers be anything/anyone but me? I see me walking toward me. I see <u>three</u> me's walking toward me. There once was an old-world farmer named Henbro Hikk who was all the time saying, "Everyone in the world is me."

+

They're *not* three me's. I know you knew that, but have you figured out yet who the thoroughly white-haired ones are? I'll bet you haven't.

+

I haven't either. So I'll go on to something else.

The mists of antiquity?

No, much too vague.

Volume?

No, that's too indeterminate a topic, too many definitions.

Fly mold?

Obviously, no.

I take another peek—the three still look like me. They're now halfway across Pine Street.

Why is the bottom floor of the building behind me empty?

The triangular phalanx of Jolty Jone look-a-likes floats right by me and into the building. Didn't they see me standing here?

+

It's been a long time since I looked at myself in a mirror. So it's altogether possible that those people maybe did not look all that much like me. Three heads of white hair, yes. But I think that some people just get white hair as they age. Do we then have three older people walking in tight formation into the building that's supposed to belong to me? The lead white-head unlocked that door so quickly he could well have put in enough time practicing unlocking doors to make him a candidate for age-induced white hair. The two people behind him were women, I think. They were all three about the same tall. Rei called my hair bloodless. But I would call the hair of that sweet white woman with orange freckles and azure eyes—was her name Zole? I would call her beautiful crystal hair bloodless. But it's been a long time since I've looked at myself in a mirror.

I knew you'd eventually ask that again, so I've kept my answer on the ready. The color of the skin under my white fur is green. Fresh-leaf green.

What color were the skins of the white-heads? Comparing his skin to his hair, I will label the lead male as a middle-to-light pink. Woman number one was so very dark brown that her skin looked truly black against her white hair. Woman number two—*one* and *two* are not names nor parts of names that I'm assigning to these women—was honey colored.

Right now I'm thinking those three were not well-aged. I'm thinking they are white of hair from early on in their lives, just like me. And they didn't pay much attention to me because they thought I was just another of the bunch of them who are gathering for a meeting in that room. *Good thinking, Jolty. That makes perfect sense.*

So if I open the door and stick my head in, are Pink and Brown-Black and Honey going to be sitting in their neat triangle on the floor facing the door? Or the stairs? Or are they going to be nervously hovering in the air every which where? Wait! I almost forgot. They could also be squeezing and bending their bodies at various angles to fit themselves into the narrow crevices between the sound absorbers that I at first took for alien life-forms lining the walls. Or they could have gone on upstairs. By now, if they were so inclined, they could be up there hanging comfortably by their heels from the rafters. Or they could be jumping up and down, higher and higher on that bed until they crash through the skylight and escape. Escape what?

If there's going to be a big meeting, perhaps I should wait out here until everyone arrives. What about Jane and Rei?

"Hello."

No. It can't be. Not again. There's someone behind me.

I lace my fingers irregularly together on top of my head.

I surely wish I knew who is back there. Without me having to turn around.

"Is there anyone inside yet?"

I'm going to find that it's a white haired person standing behind me. I know it. Someone with white hair and a female voice, a birdy voice.

I was wrong. It is a woman all right but with tawny hair.

I have no more than turned to face her hair when she starts jumping up and down and clapping her hands. "You're Jolty Jone!"

"Yes, you are correct. I am Jolty Jone." My voice has diamond sand in it. "Who are you, and how do you know my name?"

Her head jerks to the side as if I have slapped her face.

I take one step back so that she won't feel so threatened by me.

She turns fidgety. "Why are you out here? Why

aren't you inside?"

"I like being outside is why I'm out here." I tip my head at her. "And I like being outside is why I'm not inside."

She smiles at that.

"Tippi Fawn."

I reserve judgment.

"That's my name. Tippi Fawn. It is not a description of my personality."

"I will try to remember that."

Who am I kidding? I will not remember this person five minutes after she's out of my sight. (Hah! I said that as if it's not true of everybody and anything.)

"I have never met a really important person before."

Tippi the fawn was looking me *so very deep* in the eyes as she told me that. I look her back in the eyes and say…something. Something stupid. "I've never met anyone important, either."

That sentence of mine is stupid mainly because I don't know if it's for real or not. I don't care if it's for real or not. All I wanted to do with it was to demonstrate to the woman facing me how stupid her sentence sounded.

"Jolty!"

That's a somewhat familiar voice. I turn my head ninety degrees—there's Jane coming across Pine Street. This time she's wearing a violet one-piece suit and shiny black shoes. That's not the way she was dressed when she left the building this morning. Perhaps I'm going to have to follow her someday to find out where she keeps these outfits.

Jane has been walking briskly and is a bit breathy

when she takes me by the arm. Tippi the fawn bows her head. I get the sneaky feeling that Tippi Fawn has lowered her gaze in deference to Jane. Is Jane the important person that Tippi was referring to?

I don't know what to tell you now. Something is happening, but I am not wanting to be a part of it. I could just walk away from here into forever. Or I could turn into a blanket again. Or I could be the bird that perches up on the skylight.

"Have you met Tippi, Jolty? She is one of your admirers."

"Yes, Jane," says Jolty from many miles away. "She told me her name and that it is not a description of her personality and that she has never met a really important person before. Since you already know her name, it stands to reason that she was not talking about you."

"Tippi was undoubtedly talking about you, Jolty. You *are* a very important person."

I'm confused. I tell Jane so. "I don't know what that means."

Tippi chirps, "You have had a tremendous effect on many people's lives."

I can't deal with this. Why are they doing this to me? What do they want from me? I cannot be who they think I am. For I am only a minor deity, the deity of chlorophyll. I am no one *important*.

Important is as important is, I always say. I must be important to the bacteria in my stomach. Right? Are these two women and maybe the three white-heads inside the building more of my bacteria? Now that's a possibility! Perhaps I could find an antibacterial pill lying around here, and be done with all this.

Or! That woman (Madeleine Phitt) could come strolling by here and clandestinely slip me a throb. —But what good would a dozen throbs of my body followed by a warm glow do? None, of course. (If *none* is *not one* condensed, what is *nope*? *Not a hope*?)

I find that I have nothing more to say on the matter of Tippi and Jane and Rei and Hossmattcha and Madeleine and the sun and the moon and the stars at night. Pickles and blood.

+

She rolls over to drop off the side of her bed onto the garish oval rug that was woven for her grandfather by two silent people on the other side of the world. Her index finger traces the letters of the word camouflaged in the rug's waves of brilliant color. *Fullblood*. She remembers the feeling of every bone of her body breaking. This quiets Claire. *I'm going to have to be more careful with this life. It's not as uncomplicated as it looks.*

+

Zole is standing in their kitchen, gazing at the palm of her hand. Felix is sitting out on their porch, staring at their garden.

+

A silver coin. On the concrete at my feet. I am afraid to bend over to examine the coin more closely, afraid that the head on the coin is mine.

-15-

IF NOT A FOREST

I picture a tree and see a forestry. You ask me how? Well, *tree* leads me to *try* and *poe-tree* leads to *poe-try* and *foe-tree* leads to *foe-try* and *fo-res-tree* leads to a *for-es-try*. Just like that.

Lying like a stick on a blue lake, the left half of me in the water, the right half of me in the sky, I sing a duck song. (I found that I had to raise the left half of my mouth out of the water to sing the duck song.)

I am now again with one eye above and one eye below the blue water line. A tiny fish swims up close to my face. To see if I am edible? He pushes his little mouth against my cheek. And—whip! whip!—he has turned in an instant and is gone.

I called the water line *blue*, like the lake is blue. But more likely the line is black. (I know! I know! It's the *water/air* line. And as is true of many lines, this line has no thickness; so it can't be a color.) Black or blue or uncolored? The choice is yours.

If not a forest. If not a blue lake, is this a bed? A bed under a skylight in a room with four walls and six windows? No, that's completely impossible. I ran away from that building to never return. This is a lake in a forest under a blue sky.

The forest. Examining the forest, I see the individual trees and bushes and such. They are alive and well. But then I see them again, in a different way. I see them all as shadows on the wall, on the walls, the four walls. So was I wrong? This wouldn't be the first time, I assure you.

It's neither a blue lake in a forest nor a bed in a room. I don't know where I am, but I'm not in water or a bed. Am I lying down, like I thought I was? I really can't tell. I could be lying down or standing up. I can't tell which way gravity is pulling on me.

16

THE PULL OF GRAVITY

I like that. THE PULL OF GRAVITY. I don't know if gravity actually *pulls*. I have a feeling that most people in the know would use some form of the word *attract* instead of *pull*, as if there is a difference. "Gravity: terrestrial gravitation as modified by the centrifugal force due to the earth's rotation." I watched someone write that on a chalkboard somewhere in my life. I'm seeing at this moment that if I were without gravity, I would not *know* anything. Nothing at all. No forms would form, no colors would color, no memory would remember, no existence would exist.

That's all fine and well, but I am apparently without gravity right now. Form and color and memory and existence—how long before they all vanish? That is probably another stupid question, for time is obviously totally dependent on gravity, too. Hey ho! Why don't I just turn myself over/around and see what happens? Nothing.

Nothing happened. So have I finally made it into the forever world, the mind-only world? (The word *world* was clearly an unfortunate choice there.)

It suddenly occurs to me that I am not hearing anything.

Then I *am* hearing things, all kinds of little things.

Then I know I am lying down.

Then I know my eyes are closed.

Then I open my eyes.

I see a face.

It's Jane Hupiter's face.

It's gazing serenely down at me.

I may be feeling a need for more information. I search a larger area of the picture presented to me.

Jane's dark hair is pulled back and most likely bunched up at the rear of her head. She appears to have on another one of those one-piece suits, a bright aqua-green number this time. I see behind her another face. It's Rei. And now I make out a third face. It's that woman, Tippi Fawn. Tawny haired Tippi Fawn.

Jane speaks. "Hello there."

Rei speaks. "Welcome back."

Tippi just smiles.

All three are standing, looking down at me.

One could randomize the whole scene and make it a not-colorable item. Or, Jolty Jone, one could try an equal mix of morbid and mordant voices in a simplemindedly humorous package. Implore Jane and beseech Rei— gloomily, bitingly, gruesomely, caustically. Ignore Tippi, for now. "Where am I and what happened? Take me to your leader! What time is it? Has everybody gone home already?" Yes, I had no problem remembering my name and no special wish to not be able to remember it.

"You are in your building, Jolty." Jane's voice is dancing like a tall, single flame. "Look around. Don't you remember this room?"

I do. I'm lying in the middle of the floor of the big empty room.

Scanning the room the best I can without raising my shoulders from the floor, I fail to locate the three white-heads. I expected them to be levitating high in the dim corners like bats.

"Your next question, Jolty, was 'what happened?'"

"Yes, Jane, I think you are correct."

"You collapsed right in front of us on the sidewalk. One second you were standing, next second you were on the ground, dear."

Dear? Am I a *dear*? Why did Jane slip in that stupefying word?

It's Rei's turn. "I thought you had died," she says, curling her lips at the word *died*.

Jane crowds back in. "But Tippi checked you out and said you had only fainted."

My eyes sink into Tippi's waiting eyes. Yes, there is enough empty space back, down in there behind her eyes that she could have checked me out like Jane said. She, Tippi, would have thought she was really doing something. She's a mixed-up kid and doesn't know it.

Who *isn't* "a mixed-up kid and doesn't know it"?

If you are a mixed-up kid and do know it, you're COOL. If you are not a mixed-up kid and don't know it, you probably don't exist. Or you are a salad green. If you are not a mixed-up kid and do know it, you spell trouble.

"Next you commanded Rei and Tippi and me to take you to our leader." Jane pretends to cough into her hand. "We don't actually have a leader."

Now what does that mean, they don't *actually* have a leader?

"And then you asked what time is it."

That was Tippi. Tippi spoke.

Back to her I say, "And what time is it, dear?"

"It is a quarter past five."

"That's the first five after noon, not the first five after midnight?"

"Yes."

"On the same day that you and I first met?"

"Yes, it's still the same day we finally met."

Rei impolitely breaks into Tippi's and my private conversation. "Everybody else has left, yes."

Everyone else? What kind of question will I have to put together to find out who *everyone else* was and why they came here in the first place? If I keep the question plain and straightforward, I could speak with the maddening subtlety of a language without vowels—and that might steer one of these three women to an immediate and useful answer. "Wh ws vrn ls nd wh dd thy cm hr n th frst plc?"

They were listening. I could see they were all intently listening.

Surprise! Tippi is the first one to understand my question.

"Jolty Jone is wanting to know," says Tippi to Jane while Tippi is holding onto Jane's arm the way Jane has held onto my arm (of course I am still flat on my back on the floor), "who was here and why did they come."

"They came to see the famous Jolty Jone." Jane gets her slyer-than-sly look in her eyes as she tells me, "The Trinity were here, the Baabs were here, the Names and Numbers were here...etc....twenty-five or thirty people, I'd say." She remembers something and laughs. She softly kicks the side of my leg with her shoe. "All humans like you."

Pushing myself up to rest on my elbows, I ask another dangerous question, this time *with* vowels. "They've never been here before, Jane?" I'm ready to counter with the fact that that one white-head unlocked the door so quick and easily.

"They have each and all been here many times before." Jane lifts Tippi's hands off of her arm and then kneels beside my head. "But out of today's group, Jolty, only Rei and I had been in this building *with you* before this afternoon. Everyone else today is fairly new. They all first came here after you left."

I remember that singer in the trees. What was it he said? *I have seen many pictures of Jolty Jone. All of us have.* A dozen words intact in my memory. Utterly confident, I say, "Do you have a picture of me, Jane?"

"Not on my person, Jolty, not right now. There are some in that cabinet upstairs, but you have undoubtedly already seen those."

No. I have not looked inside any of the storage places up there, except to a limited extent that old wardrobe where my clothes are. Was I supposed to peek inside every space and container? I guess I was, seeings as everything up there is supposedly all mine, except for Jane and Rei's suitcases *under* the bed. Investigate—that's probably what they expected me to do the times they left me there alone. "Be curious," they should have said just before they went out the door. Then I might have gotten the point. But probably not. Even now, I don't have any interest in combing through that room.

Smug.

There's that word again. I'd like to be able to use the word *smug* every now and then, but I never remember that the word exists until I see it in print. And then I can never find any place to use the word before I forget it again. *Smug* would frequently be useful in describing certain human tendencies.

There's another word too... I've thought of it several times lately. What is it? *Hargent*. It could be someone's name or it could be a regular self-describing noun (better known perhaps as a common noun or a concrete noun). Every time I have thought of the word *hargent*, maybe a minute after that, I think of the sentence *Healthy survive and are visible*. The word and the sentence seem to go together, although I have no idea why.

Why did *smug* occur to me here and now? And without my seeing it in print. Jane and Rei and Tippi are a bit glossy, but they aren't acting smug, not any more than just about everyone does. These three women could even appear now and then in the same sentence and not clash ominously with each other. And they have! Sooner or later the explanation of why the *smug* word paid me this visit will make itself obvious.

I can understand—I don't truly understand but I am pretending for now that I do—that lots of people want to have more than one picture taken of themselves over a period of time. Yet, even so, however, still, I was upset by a perfect stranger saying to me that he and others like him have seen *many* pictures of Jolty Jone, me.

And! Do these pictures show me as green of body? I think probably not. People say things to me like "there is no one else in the WholeWideWorld who looks like you," and "you are not that hard to unmistakably describe," but no one ever wants to discuss my greenness with me. Except...I am remembering now a woman named Mimi Reams who painted herself entirely green, perhaps so that she would look like me. Even now, I hear her saying to me that I have to find my answer myself. And she also said that when I could tell her my name, then we would talk, her and I. Well, I can tell her my name now, where is she?

Why don't I just ask Jane and get the suspense over with? "Jane?"

"Yes, Jolty?"

"Do you see me as green?"

"Are you asking if I see your skin as being green?"

"That is precisely what I am asking. Yes."

Is she answering me? She's looking right at me, but I am not hearing anything. Maybe I should turn off my protection. (You know, the change I made in the position from which I talk inside, the way that I keep Jane and Rei from hearing my thoughts. I assume it also prevents me from hearing their thoughts.) Jane could be talking to me right now from inside her brain. No! I really don't think turning off my protection is a good idea. Let Jane answer me out loud. What does she have to lose? Rei can undoubtedly hear Jane's thoughts anyway. Can Tippi? Maybe Tippi is the problem.

Jane is still staring forthright into my eyes. Oops! So is Rei. And oops again. So is Tippi.

"You are green, Jolty."

She finally said the words, Jane did. She said I am green.

+

But when I climb to my feet, Jane quickly says, "How you look to me—to us—is wholly dependent on how you think you look to us. There is no you except the one that you have chosen for yourself from among all the possibilities afforded by this incarnation of yours. And the you that you are choosing for today may not be the same you that you chose yesterday. So I—we—might be a bit slow in perceiving how you are appearing today."

Sounds to me. Sounds to me like she's backpedaling. I think she's taking back now what she said right before I stood up. I can feel fourteen rivers cascading through her head, all twisting and turning every which way. "So you didn't see me as green until I asked if you did. Am I right, Jane?"

"Rei and I have been trying to see you as green all along, Jolty, ever since our and your old friend Mimi Reams told us that she had spotted you from a distance and saw that you were seeing yourself as green. That's why she shaved her head and painted herself green—emerald green, as I remember—before she ventured out on that path to talk with you."

"But you don't actually see me as green yourself. Am I right, Jane?"

I could have been beating this woman with a horsewhip; she looks so pained and distressed. Rei too. And Tippi too but not quite so much.

"Why did you disconnect from Rei and me the morning after we brought you back here to your building, Jolty?"

"I didn't like the two of you eavesdropping on my thoughts, Jane Hupiter."

"You taught us the beauty of being constantly in contact."

"I don't remember doing that."

"Jolty?" Rei wants to say something. She can't. Instead she raises her blouse to bare the long scar below her breast, the scar that I said I remembered when she showed it to me before, under the tree that I had climbed up in to die. She has no trouble saying, "You did that."

I involuntarily responded again to the scar on Rei's body, but I had and have not a single image of me causing that scar. I need to cough. I bark it out loudly without covering my mouth. "I don't remember doing that."

Harehearted as I am, you are surely wondering what I will do in such a situation. Watch. I am walking toward the door. I reach the door and turn the handle. Are the great seven seas waiting on the other side of the door to come crashing in on me? Nope.

The sidewalk outside the door is deep grey in the late afternoon—this is where I fell to the cement? But the sun is shining nicely on Pine Street. A dog is sitting out in the middle of the brightly lit street watching me.

Wisdom is the display of wisdom. An hour earlier, a day later, I am back up in my tree, my "tree to die in." Jane and Rei and Tippi sat on the ground under the tree all night long and much of the morning, but they are gone now. I'm alone again, having long forgotten (until now) that I at first mistook this tree for my Hossmattcha-watching tree. Which is of course gone. That tree. Which is of course...which is and was of course gone.

17

OMINOUS MONOTONY

My reuse of the word *ominous* so quickly must be significant. Right? *Ominous* is not like *smug*. *Ominous* has meat on it, meat and muscle and spit, while *smug* just hangs there like an empty balloon. Mimi's eyes are dark brown, vividly dark brown. The sun is an eerie fading orange. The many long leaves near my face are sledgehammer-green. That's a color I just made up. *Sledgehammer green* wouldn't work very well as the name of a color for the general p., but it fits what I am perceiving right now. It—this is a new *it*, different from the *it* in my last sentence—is easier all the way around living in a tree. On an evening like this one, it's absolutely marvelous to live in a tree. And no one has bothered me at all for maybe a week now. Just me and the tree and the sky and the grass below. Food? Food and water? Since you asked, I'll tell you. Every morning when I wake up, there is a covered plate of food and a round jar of fruit juice on a tray wedged between the tree's trunk and its first big branch. You will immediately ask how the tray gets there. And I will tell you immediately right back that I don't know. Nor do I care. It's just there in the morning, and I don't have to climb all the way down to the ground to get it. Naturally things happen when one eats food and drinks water. I'm not talking about staying healthy and all that. I'm referring to waste products. The body's throwaways. Have no fear. I quickly found a solution to the waste problem and have had it in operation for nearly as long as I've been up here. I won't be discussing it right now, being an overripe topic and all; but we will get to it eventually. Why did I bring it up if I'm not willing to discuss the matter? Oh, I was just trying to give you a more complete vision of where I am and what I'm doing. As if you care. As if I care. Come to think of it, maybe the *smug* word was meant for me. Could be. So maybe it's time for me to descend to the land and take a walk. Could be. It could be time for almost anything under our nearly gone sun.

A little globe of hate. A sphere about the size of a cow's eyeball. This glowing bubble of agitated/agitating emotion is hanging in the air out in front of me, below me, between me and the ground. It's giving off a sound…like the beat of the surf off in the distance, over a cliff and down to the sea. I try and focus my hearing on the sound coming from the bubble. The sound is a tiny voice. The bubble is saying over and over, "The mind is complete, the mind is done." If my mind is done, why is it so active? I have to admit that it keeps telling me basically the same old garbage, but my mind is active. Perhaps, just perhaps, if I could put an end to the repetitiveness, I might find that my mind is complete. But then, why would hate be telling me this?

Bang! Bang!

Someone is knocking on my tree. I look to see who. Or whom. In my biggest, baddest, most gnarly voice I say, "Who is that down there beating on my tree?"

"It am I, dearest Jolty."

There's that *dear* word again, expanded somewhat. Suffixed. I look down, and who do I see? I don't know. It's another creature from out of the ether, yet another unknown person who knows my name.

From up here it looks like the person below me has

a big *A* on his or her face. The right end of the center crossbar of the capital *A* is right between the tall-looking person's manganese-blue eyes. Probably the *A* is just an evening shadow. But it could easily be a birthmark. Or a brand. Or a tattoo. Or makeup. Or dirt. Or millions of microscopic insects. Or crossed lashes on one of my eyelids. Or a secret message being projected to me in reversed light. Where would this message be coming from? I glance up at the sky.

"I have come from afar to view my lovely friend Jolty."

It am I, the smart-aleck, who replies ironically from up in the tree with just the barest hint of the lilt heard in the voice from below, "Are you viewing this friend of yours now?"

The "blond beast" says sweetly back to me, "Must you be evasive, Jolty? I have truly come a long way to see you."

There's that *ev* word again. Rei called me that, Jane called me that, and here is this tallish, short-hair blonde with big lips using the word on me. Should I just ignore the word, or should I actually hear it. I'll take a middle ground and hear the word but pay it little mind. That sounds safe enough to me, as long as I'm up out of reach here in my tree.

+

Which wasn't much longer. I soon descended from my throne, my throne of death. The man is not so tall as he looked from up in the tree. I think his not-missing-anything gaze had made his face seem closer. Do you remember that nice woman named Zole and the man named Felix? The blond beast that had called me down from my tree told me he had learned where to find me from Zole and that Zole and Felix had been bringing the food and drink to me every morning. And the *A* no longer showed on the man's face. When I asked him about the *A*, he said that people (many people or only a few?) have told him they sometimes see the letter on his face but most of the time they can't find it there. He had never seen it himself. And he didn't tell me his name for a long while. I assume he was assuming that I already knew his name and that I was only pretending I did not know it, him, or that I was his friend Jolty. He said his name is Ferrus. Ferrus Harrus. Yeah, I didn't believe him either. But given his effulgent manner, he could wear a name like that. And he told me that he and I had known each other for a long time but we had been apart for a while. When I told him I had already heard that story a number of times, he laughed merrily. This is an up guy. We walked, not talking much, well into the night. Ferrus never once brought up our past.

+

That's because he and I have no shared past to bring up. All these people...telling me things I don't remember...things that they claim are from my history. Some of the things and some of the people seem somewhat familiar, but not familiar like memory. More like prints in the sand. An imprint of a paw isn't the paw. It isn't even a memory of the paw. It's a dent in the sand made by a paw.

+

I'm lying in the bed of Ferrus Harrus. He has a nicely furnished apartment, clean and tidy yet not compulsively so. In the clear morning light I gaze from his bed out the window and across the street at the site of the now deceased Hossmattcha-watching tree. No! That's not true! Definitely not! We are in a whole different part of town than that ex-tree site. Across the street is another huge apartment building, not grass and trees. Why oh why did I say I was staring at my Hossmattcha tree?

Ferrus is in another room, the kitchen I think, fixing us something to eat. For some unknown reason I'm tempted to get up from his bed and go over and peek in his closet. Would half of the closet be filled with those one-piece suits that Jane wears? Why am I now associating Ferrus with Jane? They are two completely different types of people. And what in the world could "types of people" mean?

No, I think I'll pass up this golden opportunity for closet peeking. I will get up from here, though. Up and up. Do up! Do down. Up and down, up and down, up and down. Splack! Splack! Do the duckwalk into the toilet room. While singing in a soft voice, Interlude With a Cactus.

I spy a tiny, curtainless window on the only available wall of the tiny, cramped toilet room. The window, as I see it, looks into a shaft, a four-sided, vertical shaft, a shockingly narrow shaft, unpainted, probably open to the sky at the top. An air well! Yes, that's what this is. That's what this kind of shaft is called. Across the air well from the window is another window. Looking straight through both windows, I see Ferrus in the kitchen doing this-and-thats that befit kitchens. How long do you think I can stand here watching him through the windows before he discovers me? I open my window, reach across the shaft, and rap on his window. The air is cooler in the shaft. Ferrus springs over to his window, quickly raises it, and reaches out to take my hand.

I'm not here, even if my hand is!

Now that declaration sounded exactly like someone just being contrary.

OK. I am here, all of me. And I'm liking the feel of Ferrus's hand.

I use the toilet, then coltwalk back into the bedroom to find my clothes and get dressed. Fully attired, I amble leisurely, nonchalantly into the kitchen. The kitchen table wasn't seeable through the two windows. At the table sits Jane Hupiter, openly smiling at me. I immediately spin about and return to the bedroom. I stride straight to the closet, throw open its doors, and behold a whole slew of those colorful one-piece rigs. The closet is simply brimming with the seductive smell of Jane. Around and around and around. Bang, bang, someone's knocking on my tree.

+

At least I was fully dressed when I ran out of there. Dressed and done and gone away. Slip, slip, slipping away. I wish I would find Mack right about now. Or anyone else who's not so scattered as the people I've been thrown into the arms of recently. Those blinking scatterbrains!

Hah! Who am I trying to kid! No one could be more scattered than Mack March. His brain (or something) has him continuously heading out every which way at once.

Certainly it would make no sense at all for me to return to my throne of death. Maybe I will just turn left and go as far as I can in that direction, then turn right, go as far as I can that way, then turn left…etc. Where would I end up? Boy, I hope not at the now famous ex-tree site. I've had enough of even just thinking about that place. What say we head for the frontier and break into new territory?

And which way would that be? I bet I could walk in any one direction all day and all night and still not reach a limit of this city. I foresee endless trudging thisaway and thataway over the earth, but where else is there for me to go in search of "the frontier"? I've already done up, as in up in a tree. How about underground? That one I've never tried. But the only way down—that I've ever heard of around here—is in the utility pipes, and they don't go down but a short way. And how could a mostly level pipe lead to a frontier? It couldn't. No, that's silly to even think about.

I always say, if you can't locate any new territory, go sit by the biggest body of water you can find. But the biggest body of water I can find is usually another person.

Now with all that having been said, let us get serious.

Get it? "Let us get serious." No? You still don't get it? No matter, it was lame anyway. In fact, now that I think about it, it was entirely a personal pun. There is no way you could have gotten it. Sorry about that. Or if you did get it, you must have gotten something else that was hidden in there. Or if you somehow got the same thing I intended for you to get—wow!

Peas and pipes. Or would that be P's and pipes? Whatever. Walking, walking, walking. It's still fairly early in the morning I think. I'm whipping down the avenue, free as a bird. No, wait a second. From what I've observed of birds, they are no more free as a species than the humans are— Oh! Right! Everybody already knows that. I'll lip my zips.

See, I actually could keep myself from talking/thinking. It's maybe noon or a little after now. I'm still walking, but it's been at least a couple of hours since you've heard from me. The answer to that is no. I have not been jotting down rackle-tackle to think/talk about later, either. Later being sometime in the future. It's been purely quiet inside here, like a lake that's so clear you can't be sure it's there, real relaxing, the prime stuff of the super beings of all the species. When the feets get tired, however, it's time to pause in our journey.

Hah! Where am I? Have I ever been in this locale before? Doesn't seem so. Seems all new to me. Looks like the bare bottom of the universe, in fact. Get a grip, I tell myself. Those two big humps over there are some kind of stadium or something, not a giant butt. And they're not just right across the street, they're away in the distance. Optical illusion, you know.

"Hello, Jolty Jone."

Here we go again! Somebody behind me who knows my name! I won't reply to them or turn to look. I'll just stand here, pausing in my journey.

"How's the green one among us today?"

Today? This person knew before today that I'm

green? I have to look. And I do. And it's Mimi Reams behind me. I would have guessed it was her. Then I realize that she herself could have been "the green one among us today," except this time, today, there's no emerald paint covering her skin.

And she's no longer bald. Her hair is growing out. It's maybe as long as my thumb. I say to her, "I can tell you my name now."

"Of course you can: I just said it to you."

She's still smaller than me, though. "But I could have told you even if you hadn't said it first."

"That's good news, Jolty."

"I still want to know why I knew your name the last time we met, Mimi? And why did you know that I knew your name?"

"You can remember the last time we met, Jolty?"

"As if it were five minutes ago."

"Fine. We can talk now."

"Did you follow me here, Mimi?"

"I could ask you the same question. This is where I work, Jolty. This is my café."

We *are* standing out in front of a café. The sign over the door reads THE CLAIRE FULLBLOOD CAFÉ. And under that, in smaller letters, NEAR MOSS AND MIMI REAMS, PROPRIETORS.

I'm sinking through the sidewalk. I'm riding a slow elevator down. I'm going underground. Death has finally come for me.

"Why don't you come on in and sit down, and I'll bring you some food."

"OK," was my weak reply.

+

"Let me give it to you in a tidy little package. Do you recognize the name Claire Fullblood, Jolty?"

"As if from out of a dream, Mimi, yes."

"Claire was your mother."

"What?"

"She died giving birth to you."

"I…"

"Near Moss was not your father. He never once laid eyes on you. Certainly Ridge is your father. Whether he has ever seen you I don't know. Probably he has not. Probably he is not even aware you exist. I'm assuming he is still alive somewhere. Near Moss died not long ago. He lived a life filled with grief, after your mother left him."

"Why am I called Jolty Jone and not something-or-other Ridge? Or Fullblood?"

"You were adopted by an otherwise childless couple, older people. They named you. Jone is or was their last name. I don't know if they are still alive or not. Probably they are."

"How do you know all this, Mimi?"

"Near cried here alone in this café for years, until I bought into the place. He then had my tender young shoulder to cry on. Soon I was spending most of my free time searching for Claire Fullblood, his long lost love. Maybe I could talk her into coming back. It took me a good-sized chunk of time, but eventually I found her. That is, I discovered where Claire had died quite some time before. From there I found you living with mister and madam Jone. That's how you first knew my name. I have never located Certainly Ridge. And I never told Near about you."

"Am I green?"

"You are truly green, Jolty."

18

THAT'S HOW YOU FIRST KNEW MY NAME

My, she is pleasing to look at. She said we were born on the same day, same day and same year. We are exactly the same age. Her mother died before she got to know her, too. Just like me. We could have been twins, except we were born at opposite ends of town and had different mothers. Her mother was not alone when she died, as mine was. Mimi's father is still alive and doing well, she says.

All that is nice. Homey et al. But everything Mimi has told me—it still doesn't feel to me like it actually has anything to do with me. Am I stuck in a parallel reality? It seems quite possible that I am. No, it seems more and more *likely* that I am. Nonetheless, I enjoy being here with Mimi. I just listen to her and don't say a thing myself that might spoil our rapport.

The café got busy; so Mimi had me move into the kitchen. I'm leaning back against a painted brick wall on a rickety old wooden chair, staring at a sign hanging high up out of the way above a pair of big, deep sinks. Steel sinks. REMEMBER THE DOG. Whatever that means. Twisting the words and letters of the sign around, I try to make them into something new and cuter. Alas, I admit defeat. Yes, I should simply be shot for failing at so basic a task.

"Whatcha thinking about, Jolty"

Mimi is back from the front momentarily.

"How much I like you, M."

"Good. Bye, kid."

Mimi is out in front from the back again.

Who is THE DOG? Me? Has Mimi kept that sign hanging up there to remind her to think about me? No-o-ope, I don't think so. A woman like Mimi has got many more and better things to think about than me. I'm sure.

She's back again. She looks a bit frazzled. She must have been awfully young when she "bought into" this café. With her father's help? Can one really own (or partly own) a business at that age? I ask her if I can help. She asks if I would like a job working here with her. I don't know what I am thinking when I say yes.

+

"That house over there was your mother's, Jolty. She gave it to Near Moss just before she left him. Near didn't want it without her. He had as little to do with that house as possible. When he died he willed it to some charitable institution. They're using it for their headquarters now."

"I thought we were going to your abode, Mimi."

"I just brought you this way so that you could see the house."

"A house I never lived in."

"Right. You are so right, Jolty. My place is not far, just a couple more blocks on down this street. We will go home by a different route tomorrow."

I have a secret I shant tell Mimi. I could draw for her the complete layout of the inside of that big house. Right here and now. I could describe to her the colors and design of the bathroom tiles. I could sketch the giant scenes (once) painted on the walls. Have they been painted over?

No, I don't want to know!

It's late. It's dark. We are walking to Mimi's house from the closed café. Mimi says, "That is where I live. There." She points at a dark space in the night. I know I will lose my greenness if I stay too long with Mimi and work in her café. I decide to not think about that little fact. Except…I wonder if Mimi is aware of this, my predicament. She turns on every light in the compact, cozy, convenient, intimate house. "Home!" she exclaims. "And next, a bath."

We are in the bathtub laughing and splashing each other. She is so pretty. Yes, I'm thinking about it again. No one ever refers to me as *he* or *she*. If I have no gender, what am I? Yes, I remember me saying that I am the green deity up in a tree. But I am no longer up in a tree. If I stay with Mimi will she make me into a man or woman? Would she make me a man, or would she make me a woman? Or do things not work quite like that? I decide to not think about that little question.

Mimi stands up in the tub. "And next, to bed."

She made me into a man. Yep. She had the knowledge and the skill, and she made me into a man, a man I liked. A man she liked, too, I'm pretty sure. I didn't ask her if she is planning to change me into a woman tomorrow night. Let it lie, I always say.

That was the longest night I ever experienced. After Mimi and I relaxed at last and let go of each other and closed our eyes to sleep, dreams came pouring in. Confusing dreams, scary dreams, lonely dreams, fantastic dreams, slick dreams, ragged dreams, ugly dreams, and on and on. This morning, sitting up in bed, I remember nothing of the dreams. I remember only the categories I filed the dreams into. Categories—are they the friend that is actually the enemy?

I am up. Up on my feet. Feets are down on the floor. There is adequate light in here to see most everything; still the sun is far from up. Mimi is in the bathroom brushing her teeth. I can see the back of her through the open door. She looks at me in her mirror. Quickly I assume a flamboyant pose beside the bed. I did indeed mean to say *flamboyant*: I can see most of me in that mirror, and I look very much like an unflickering flame in form and color. In color, you ask? Yes, just one afternoon and night have passed in this new life, and this morning I am not green. When did I cross the frontier and enter this new territory? I don't really know; but if anyone ever asks me, I'll unabashedly say that it was yesterday, when I told Mimi I would work with her in her café.

+

"You shouldn't stare at the customers, Jolty. Most people don't like to be stared at."

"Sorry. Was I staring, Mimi? Of course I was if you say I was. Why is it that people do not like to be stared at?"

"Usually, I think, it's because they can't figure out why you are so interested in looking at them."

"But it is all right if they stare at me?"

"They will get used to you pretty soon, partner?"

I can't decide if Mimi was purely joking with the tag *partner*. "Why don't I get to look until I get used to them?"

"They are the customers. They pay money to come in here and have their privacy respected."

"In other words I am a paid entertainer."

Mimi slips over beside me just long enough to pat me lovingly on the head and say, "Working here might seem like that to you for a while."

It does.

Who is that out on the sidewalk with their face pressed to the glass to see in here? Jane? Yes, and that's Rei behind her. What do they want? Me, of course.

They are not coming inside. Will they wait out there until the café closes and then ambush me while I'm walking home with Mimi? Wait! Jane is signaling for me to come out there.

"Don't go out there, Jolty."

"Why not, Mimi?"

"They will tell you things, and you will never come back in here."

"What things will they tell me?"

"Whether they tell you or I tell you, it makes no difference. You won't stay with me any longer."

"Do you expect me to choose to remain ignorant of what Jane and Rei have to tell me and just stand here allowing your customers to stare at me until they tire of doing so?"

"Yes. We are partners, aren't we?"

She's serious about us being partners. "Yes. OK."

+

"Evelyn? Evelyn Singer?"

I turn away, not answering the woman. I saw her come in fastidiously attired in a flowing silver dress, brief turquoise cloak and wide purple hat. Was she talking to me or to a private ghost of hers?

Mimi steps to the counter and says straight to her face, "No, this is Jolty Jone."

"Oh!" The woman abruptly spins away from Mimi and me. She spots a table over by the window and beelines to it.

Mimi gives me a sign that she will wait on the woman. So I take a break and slip out to the sidewalk.

Here I am in the sunshine, and I'm remarkably at ease. Mimi is easy to live with. But where do I go from here? I could climb up on the roof of Mimi's house and not come down until the buzzards have eaten my body and my ghost could then safely descend to the city and proceed to the house that Mimi said once belonged to a woman named Claire Fullblood, who was also said by Mimi to be my died-at-my-birth mother, which can't be true because I once saw this Claire Fullblood standing under my death tree looking up at me and calling "Certainly" as if she wanted someone other than me to answer her by climbing down from the tree to embrace her.

Someone is coming up the sidewalk pretending to not notice that I am standing here. It is no one I know. But just as this person is passing in front of me, a hand shoots out to force a slip of paper on me. The person neither stops nor says a word, and I'm left with the paper.

On the paper is a handwritten note that says in six lines: "Blue girl / blue balling black dead slender mother / lower to the ground than me / your man / your big stick fat mothering man / came from miles away to watercolor your world."

192

"Give me that!"

That same person is back, apparently demanding to have the note returned. I am slow to act, and the paper is roughly grabbed from out of my hands. The person tells me accusingly, "That's not for you," then turns and speeds away.

Whoever that was is right. There's no way that I'm a "black dead slender mother."

Did this most recent incident strike you as strange or maybe even contrived? Then let me tell you about a perturbingly similar happening just yesterday. That time I didn't even get to see the perpetrator. I discovered the note on the counter beside some money a customer had left for me. I'm sure the customer had not left the note too. I had gone into the back for just a second; and when I returned, the note was there. This note was very anonymously machine-printed. "In case you haven't figured it out yet," the note read, "you can't be a man, even if *she* wants you to be. What she is wanting is for you to be the (natural) father and her the mother of Zole."

Ka-a-bang! My head exploded.

It then exploded again. Could the note have been referring to the same Zole who comes to my mind?

Not an hour later—I almost forgot this part—a second note was left on the counter. Same kind of machine printing. "Neither can you be a woman. Your *wants*, what you have of *wants*, are all wrongly pointed."

After I found and had read the first note, I didn't know what to do with it. After I had found and read the second note, I decided to act courageously and show them both to Mimi, later, after work. I would have asked her to translate the messages for me on our way home last night—if the two slips of paper had not mysteriously disappeared from the shelf in the café where I had laid them. Even so, the vanishing of the slips of paper is no excuse. I remembered exactly what the notes said and certainly could have relayed their contents to Mimi. But I didn't. And today we had this give-and-takeback-on-the-sidewalk fiasco. I don't see the connection yet, yet the twin notes of yesterday and the flyaway one of today must be linked somehow. Or maybe all three notes were meant for Evelyn Singer.

I step back into the café and look for the woman in the purple hat and turquoise cloak. She is still sitting at that table by the window. She could have been watching me while I was outside. She is not even glancing at me now. I walk over to her, stand quietly beside her for a moment, and then ask her, "Who is Evelyn Singer?"

The woman unhurriedly raises her eyes to my face. She studies my face for several long seconds before smiling distantly. "You are not Evelyn Singer. You are Jolty Jone. That woman over there told me so."

"I am aware of that. But who is Evelyn Singer?"

"I am Evelyn Singer, even though I mistook you for her a few minutes ago. Forgive me, please." Her faraway smile turns down into a pained grimace, and she waves me away from her.

Mimi is up on her toes. She waves for me to come to her.

"Goodbye," says Jolty Jone in a mocking tone to a deaf ear hiding under a lurid hat.

+

Lying again on this soft comfortable bed in the near dark, I am thinking that a much higher percentage of dogs and cats than humans see the immense, closed circle of life and leaving-life and death and leaving-death (do). Do.

I am not talking until Friday night. I told—or maybe I should say *warned*—Mimi—his morning that I was not going to speak to anyone until after work Friday. Yes, I know what day it is. It's Wednesday night. Actually Thursday morning. I've come to remember the days and even the time of day, plus or minus an hour. I still totally lose the time ever so often, but with some effort on my part it does come right back to me.

I am now thinking that *time* is such a wild assumption. And supposedly everyone makes this assumption shortly after their birth. How can time be true?

No, my not-talking did not cause problems at work today. Most of the customers mistook my refusing to reply as gameplaying. Many of them joined me in the game with weird gestures of their own aplenty. Obviously, they've gotten used to me. And Mimi just smiled drolly at me whenever she wanted my attention.

She's here lying beside me right now, very much asleep. Her body is the soft, warm spaceship of the living. Whatever whatever whatever that means! Does my body feel *so real* to her? I push my nose into her hair, the stuff of dreams. I'm in a logging camp high up on the sierra with a powerful tree saw in my hands. I raise the saw high to the sky as if challenging the threatening clouds overhead to strike me dead.

"Be still, Jolty. You keep waking me up with all your moving around."

See? What I mean? The stuff of dreams.

"For time to be true, Mimi, you would have to be a tree saw."

"Huh? What are you saying? Are you awake or dreaming, Jolty?"

"Oh, I'm quite awake. Oh, I'm quite asleep."

"You are awake!" Mimi jerks the sheet up over her head.

I hear nothing more from her for the hour that I lay listening for her. At the close of that hour I realize what I have done: I have talked to Mimi. That's why she wanted to be sure I was awake. Now I'm going to have to talk to her and everyone else tomorrow.

+

Evelyn Singer said that she mistook me for Evelyn Singer. How can someone mistake someone else for themselves? Whoo! I think I might have just been sent a direct answer to that question.

Mimi and I are on our way home from work. It's dark. Mimi points over into the deeper dark beside a tall building. There is a person there. What is this person doing? Painting on the wall. Spraying paint on the wall in the dark. Mimi grabs my arm to stop me, but I shake her off and stride over to the painter.

"What are you doing there?" asks Jolty Jone ingenuously.

"What does it look like?" says the painter in a rough voice.

"I can't really say," speedily I answer. "It's too dark out here." From the voice I assume it is a man.

"I am painting my self on this wall."

"*Myself* as one word or *my self* as two words?"

"You heard correctly—two words. My self will be left on the wall when this body walks away from here."

"Oh, maybe I get it." Did I? I think I might have. "Are you attempting to gain a state of selflessness by separating your very self from your body and leaving the self behind adhering to a wall?"

"That is not the way I would have described it, but yah."

I think I saw the painter set down his paint can on the ground and pick up another.

He grunts and sighs. "I am not going to just leave it alone here forever, though. This body will return fairly often to visit its self."

"But if you are separated from your self, won't you also be separated from your will…the will to return to visit your self, for example?" I thought my question was a good one.

"I am of the mind that the will is original, built-in equipment, not an expendable accessory like the self."

Mimi is *right* behind me. She whispers to me, "Please, let's get out of here. There's nothing painted on that wall but a plus sign. I've seen this guy around before. He is a very unpredictable sort. He's maybe even dangerous."

What is Mimi afraid of? I step up and stand face-to-face with the fresh paint. Yes, I think Mimi is right. It does look like a big yellow plus sign. At least the guy has a positive attitude. No, that would be a positive self. Where his attitude is or will be, he hasn't divulged to me yet.

The painter pushes against my arm to tell me to get out of his way, please. As Mimi and I walk away, he is spraying a red outline around his plus sign.

Mimi makes no mention of either the wall or its painter the rest of our way home. So I don't either. By the time we two reach Mimi's house, my initial bit of understanding as to how Evelyn Singer could have made that mistake has vanished. I will not underestimate Mimi.

We walk into the house. Mimi takes off her clothes as the bathtub fills. She turns to face me. She is me.

"You are me, Mimi."

She grins at every wall in the room. "I am not you, Jolty. You are just overly susceptible to far-out ideas." She curls her index finger at me. "I am not you, but I would be your lover and protector forever if you let me."

"Do I need protection, Mimi?" It's dark outside the house but warm and light in here.

"Yes. Take off your clothes and get in the tub."

So why don't I just gaily ask her, while I'm tugging off my clothes as instructed, who or what I need to be protected from? People occasionally ask straight forward questions like that. I've heard them. I have also heard the askers of such questions sounding incredibly hollow. Ho, ho, ima hollow.

In the line of bubbles along the edge of the water (where the top of the water meets the inside of the tub) does weave a long, single row of tiny hieroglyphs…which, surprisingly, I can read. "If you want to hear what I'm saying, you have to hear in my every sentence more than a little camouflaged humor. I have no permanent axe to grind. I have no need for simple-minded heroics. Let's work in as many different perspectives at once as we can."

Now who could have sent me that message? The water? I *would* like to know what the water is saying. I certainly would. Does that mean then that I'll have to see a joke or hear a joke in every drop of water?

"What in the world are you looking at like that, Jolty? Is there something ugly in the bath water? Bugs or algae or something?"

"Bugs, Mimi."

Mimi comes to the rim of the tub. Clutching my arm and pressing her naked body against my side, she examines the water. I've been told that naked people have nothing to say. Yet Mimi then examines my face and asks, "It was a message, wasn't it? A message hidden in the water."

"It was a message *from* the water. We have become friends."

Mimi's face lights up. "O-o-o! Jolty Jone has Divine Water for a friend!"

"Better believe it."

"I do believe! I do believe!"

Freeing my arm and raising my hands above my head, I grandly proclaim that the time has now come for us to enter the water and bathe. Evamq.

Comes a knock on the door.

Neither of us are wet yet.

Mimi immediately makes her position clear. "I'm

not going."

Hence I have to say, "I hope you are not expecting me to answer the door. This is not my house."

When both of us try to be first into the tub, we crash into each other and fall the rest of the way in. We are gasping for air and laughing uncontrollably when the front door of the house flies open. (We can't see that door from the tub, but we hear the latch click open and then hear the door hitting the wall.) Who strides in? The cat? No, Mimi doesn't share with a cat. A raccoon? Nope. It could be a raccoon, but I'm saying that it's not because raccoons don't usually knock first. Is it Jane and Rei? Evelyn Singer? I turn my back to the bathroom door so that I won't be the first to see who is our visitor. I watch Mimi's face as she watches the door. She did say she would be my protector. Maybe it's that lonely violinist who's always standing with his instrument on the next corner down from the café. He has transported himself here to play us a lively jig as we bathe.

No such luck, as they say. We can hear someone walking around in the other room, but nobody comes into the bathroom. Will that turn out to be *nobody comes into the bathroom* or *nobady*?

The door slams. We hear no more footfalls. Mimi stands up, wraps a towel around her, and steps gallantly out of the tub. I pat her butt as she leaves me.

Thought #2: "Why do people scream when they suddenly find themselves in a terrible situation?"

Thought #3: "My eyes open as wide as they will go."

Thought #4: "Of course Mimi is never coming back to me, the same way that Claire never came back to Near. I will eventually climb out of this tub and slosh into the other room and find on Mimi's table an envelope with a note in it that says her house is now mine. The note will end with some sincere mickymack or another, a likely example of a mickymack being, "Thank you very much, Jolty."

Lo, the wrench returneth! (I couldn't call Mimi a wench even in jest.)

"Hi." I sing to her from the tub. I wrap my two dripping arms across my front and grip my shoulders. "Who was it?"

Mimi doesn't look me in the eye. She returns to the edge of the tub. She allows her towel to drop to the floor. Raising one foot higher than necessary up and over the rim, she appears to be stepping over a prickly barrier erected to prevent unwary travelers from falling off a high precipice.

She sinks until she is completely under water. Which leaves not much room for me. So I get out and dry off on Mimi's towel. At least no death bubbles are rising to the surface. But what if she totally exhaled before she got in the water? There wouldn't be any air bubbles then either. What to do! Whether to interfere. No! The choice is hers. Yes! She may be under there waiting for me to interfere.

Yo! Do I perceive a whale spout? A faithful geyser? Hurrah! Tis the second coming of Mimi.

Oh, her face looks altogether different. I would not have recognized her if I hadn't seen positively that it was her getting in the tub. "What's the matter, Mimi?" She looks absolutely dejected.

"You are going to have to leave here, Jolty. And you can't come back to the café either. —Not now! You don't have to leave right now. You can stay till tomorrow morning."

"Why do I have to go?"

"I'd rather not say." She stands up and reaches for the towel in my hand.

I pass it to her. "Is there someone in the other room?"

"No."

"Somebody left a message then?"

"Yes." She gets out of the tub and goes over to take her robe off its hook.

"Can I read it, Mimi?"

"No." She wraps the robe tightly around her. "I burned it."

"Why?"

"I didn't want you to read it, Jolty."

A plus B equals what? What? But first I have to confirm that A and B are factors in the same equation. "Did you take those two weird notes that I found left in the café?" I was going to add a time at the end of my question (eg: the day before yesterday), but I cannot remember just now how long, how many days it has been since those notes appeared and disappeared. Am I suddenly losing my newly acquired faculty for marking time?

"I did, yes. And I burned them too."

"Who is Zole?"

"Zole is my daughter, Jolty."

"*Your* daughter?"

"Yes, *my* daughter."

She's trying to hide her condition from me, but I can tell she's crying. She shoots a furtive glance at me, then leaves me all alone again in the bathroom.

I see her, stiff as an icicle lying next to me all night long on the bed and not touching me. I find my clothes, dress myself, and leave the once-friendly little house for the huge dark of night.

+

Do I feel shame? That's an interesting idea, indeed.

I like/liked Mimi. I had strange new experiences while I was with her, not the least of which was the adventure of two people trusting each other. But the world is rolling up into a ball again.

I can't say if the painter ever goes back to visit the self left on the wall. I went back to that wall, though, the very next morning after I had talked with the painter there in the dark. (Yes, it was the very next morning after I left Mimi's too, I think. Yes, I'm pretty sure about that.) The yellow and red plus sign looked great on the wall in the bright daylight. I have no idea how the painter could have done such detailed work in that dark.

Ima hollow sitting on a concrete wall. The wall runs along the outside of a walkway over a bridge. I am waiting here for the water below to speak to me. I am ready and prepared to laugh at anything it says. Will I see characters in bubbles again, or will I hear actual sounds? Or will I just hear/see absolutely, without the aid of either air or light?

-19-

THOSE IDENTICAL ONES THAT THEY ARE

What I hear after looking down long at the water is Jane coming. She's still some way off and on foot, but she's coming for me. Should I jump off this bridge into the water and float gloriously downstream while pretending I am a lost log from the high country? There are other options, obviously. I shall not make a list of them here.

Mimi keeps a thickish book on a little table beside her bed. The position of the book on the table never changes (never changed); so Mimi maybe never reads from it. I didn't ever pick up the book in my hands, but I did once pass my eyes over its title. *DODOWN DOUP: A Non-Agreed Upon Vision of the World*. With a needlessly complex title like that, the book sounded "…initially intriguing but in the end disappointing." I brought up that book of Mimi's now because…

I didn't finish that last sentence because my head had started spinning. Earlier this morning, in a whole different part of town, my eyes picked out one line from the dozen or so on an advertisement board: "60 minutes of news in an instant!" And I thought then, while I was still facing the board, that time would have me think of life as a series of instants. Yes or no, one of the instants of life just came back to me here on the bridge. Here and now, I see what I did not see the morning I was standing beside Mimi's bed reading the title of the book on the table. On the book's cover, under the title are the words "by Jolty Jone."

"Jolty Jone!"

I have tarried a tad too long. That's Jane's voice behind me. I raise myself above the concrete wall on my strong hands and arms as I push with my feet. Soon I'm out in the air on my way to the water.

The air is in my ears; then the water is in my ears. Now I can hear the water! Clearly! Life *is* all humor! Every bit of life is either ludicrous or absurdly incongruous. That that is outside of humor is not life. Therefore, since water is life, water is but "camouflaged humor." What else did those little hieroglyphs in the line of bubbles in the tub say? "Let's work in as many different perspectives at once as we can." Yes, I see the point. I do-o-o believe!

I do believe I am not in the water any longer. Where am I? The last thing I remember is seeing a clear (colorless) light that filled a great space yet shined on nothing. Hmm. I'm trying to stand up. I make it to my knees before I lose my balance and fall back to the ground. Yes, it is the ground, not a walkway and not a floor. I try again to get up, and I fall over again. The third time, I make it to my feet. I reach out to grab ahold of something to steady myself. When I glance at my hand, it's clutching a handle-like irregularity on a dark rock. A tall dark rock. I almost thought it might be Jane waiting nearby, watching me. The slender, erect rock is taller than Jane. I cough up an acre-foot of water from my lungs. Humor?

The rock is so cool and reserved that I am the first to speak. "Hello. I am said to be Jolty Jone."

The rock says nothing in return. I remove my hand from it just in case such personal contact is embarrassing the rock. Still the rock does not speak. When suddenly I hear rushing water behind me, I do not turn to look. In front of me stands the silent rock. I sit down crosslegs on the ground, still facing the rock. This rock and I have met somewhere before.

+

The first rays of sunlight strike the very top of the rock.

The curvy line dividing sunlit from unsunlit works its way down the rock, slow-dancing over the rock's undulating surface.

Ahh! Rays strike the back of my head. Then I feel them on my neck. I feel them inching down my back. I greet the rock. "Good morning."

"Good morning, Jolty."

I am grateful that the rock has chosen to speak to me.

No, I'm not! That wasn't the rock speaking. That was Jane's voice. She must be standing behind the rock.

Jane steps out from behind the rock. She's wearing her standard one-piece thing, but what makes this outfit different is that it is exactly the same blackish brown as her hair. (Rei's hair is more red and not as dark as Jane's.) Jane says in that luscious voice she often uses when greeting people, "Nice day, huh?"

"Looks like it might have been."

Did I say that? Yes, I did. Climbing to my feet after sitting in one position for so long is another major undertaking for me.

Jane swishes up to me to touch her strikingly beautiful index finger lightly to my bared collarbone. "Are you ready to go home, Jolty?"

Peering at the stone-still rock, trying to remember if my hair is yet white, I answer, "What is there for me there?" Am I regaining my greenness, or is it gone forever. And what does *forever* mean?

"You might meet the real Jolty Jone there."

"The *real* Jolty Jone?" What can I possibly say next? "Then who am...?" I press a finger to my chest just below Jane's finger.

"Who do you want to be?"

"I liked...uh...living...or staying...with Mimi."

Jane jerks her finger away from my neck and swings that hand of hers behind her back. "No, you can't go back there."

"Why not?" I've been wrong before in thinking my question is a good one.

"It's not necessary now that you know why. I thought for a while that it was, but now it's not."

If I'm not the real Jolty Jone, why did Jane greet me the way she did just a short while ago? "Good morning, Jolty," is what she said. She did not say, "Good morning, Jolty Jone #2." I take a step back from Jane. And another. And another. I'm walking backward.

"Goodbye for now," says Jane as I enter the water. I say nothing back to her. Just as my head sinks below the surface, she waves to me.

+

Here I am in J.J.'s bed in J.J.'s building dreaming of the pages inside the book *DODOWN DOUP: A Non-Agreed*

Upon Vision of the World. I start with the preface:

Here I am again, sitting at that sh-sh-shaky table pushed up against that same permanently closed window. Here I am again, looking down over my left shoulder and out the window at block after block of old rooftops. Blocks and blocks of rotting rooftops. I've been sitting on this chair at this table looking out this dirty window at the rooftops below all day every day for two years now. Frump, frump, frump. Locky, locky, locky. Which will give out first, the rigid chair or my spine?

Looking out the window is to dream, to dream with my eyes open, to dream of what my eyes are already seeing. I dream in tertiary colors of life on another planet. Each dream that I have is of a slightly different planet. Yes, I am aware that all these *other planets* are composed in my mind, in much the same way that "natural law was/is derived from the general development of mankind." Sorry about the quotes, but I can't say where in this big mind that stream of ten/eleven words came from. Let it lie, I always say.

Just a couple of examples of past dreams:

On one planet there was no sun to center on. The rooftops below me were the only observable life form and each and all of the rooftops were dimly lit from within.

On another planet in another dream, an amorphous yellow-green-red cloud high in the sky was the one and only source of light. And far below this cloud, innumerable tiny creatures (ant-like things) passed quickly between the rooftops.

My planet dreams are silent. They have no sounds. No sound, no smells, no touchy-feely. Not enough light either. There is always just that one, removed scene (the rooftops stretching into the distance from under my window) with delicate, insignificant changes made to it.

But at night I'm out of the room. I never remember leaving the room. I never remember reentering it. . . .

How could I have known all of those words to dream them? I didn't. Obviously I made up "the preface" from word one. If ever I learn that the beginning of the book that lives on Mimi's bed table is indeed the same as I just dreamed it, I will be. . .shocked. And back to back, another startling revelation: I was dreaming, yes, but not in J.J.'s bed in J.J.'s building. I was right here, dreaming that I was in that bed dreaming that I was reading those pages. I'm awake now, awake in a slightly different kind of dreaming. "Looking out the window is to dream, to dream with my eyes open, to dream of what my eyes are already seeing." That kind of dreaming.

'Cept I have no window here to be looking out of 'cept these two round holes in my skull.

Before you ask, I want you to understand that I don't know either. So I really can't help you if you don't know (for sure) where I was referring to when I said I was *right here*.

Am I correct in thinking that a person can't or

doesn't exist without a name and that two people can't have the same name at the same time in the same place? Again, that's probably common knowledge. And if it is true that a person's appearance is determined by their desires, why can I not pinpoint anywhere in me the desire to look not-like any other human. Suddenly I'm remembering the little patch of white that used to show on the ground near my head as I went to sleep. *It's dark enough now. Now I lay me down to sleep. I lay me down, but before I sleep I check the white.*

Can't say why that mysterious patch came to mind, since I'm wide awake now. Yes. And the sun's on high. Time to get up and about.

My, my! What's this?

An'r.

What do you make of that? *An'r?* That word or whatever it was? *Answer? And her?* Myself, I didn't/couldn't make anything satisfying out of *an'r.*

Look out! Cover your head; here comes another one.

Shades of Blue.

At least it was real words this time.

Shades of Blue. That must have been a song. "O-o-o / three blues make a brown-n-n / but thinking of you-u-u / I'm removed by twelve shades of blue-ue-ue...." Or something or else like that.

"Howdy."

What! That wasn't another *an'r* or *shades of blue*; that was a voice! Cranking my head this way and that, I see no one. "Who said that *howdy?*"

"It was me, surely."

I still don't see anybody or any direction that I can

safely run. Hence, I will try a callow (smarty) reply. "And where is Me?"

"I am right here."

I am getting more and more confused. "Is that the same *right here* where I am?"

"Yes. I am in the same time and space as you."

Hmm. This is absolutely terrible. How should I proceed? —Wait! I just had a flash. "Then you must be 'the real Jolty Jone.'"

"Right-o."

In another flash I see that I am like *the print*. "And you are like *the print* as seen through the other side of the paper?"

"You can understand, certainly," says the spooky voice, "that I would much rather see us as being the other way around, as *me* being the words printed in the right direction."

Till I can get this here situation ironed out, I'll address the bodiless voice as TheRealJJ, which is nothing but a thinly disguised code (ho ho) for "the real Jolty Jone." All right-o?

In my closest approximation to an ironclad voice I demand, "Did you write that *Dodown Doup* book, the one on Mimi Ream's night table?"

"I most assuredly did. And I placed the book on that table myself so that you would see it there."

Startled and splurting like a fool, I claim, "I never opened the book."

"I, of course, know that."

I may be gaining the upper hand here, as TheRealJJ is beginning to sound overly self-confident. "Am I in your book?"

"You, more than anyone else, are in the book."

What TheRealJJ needs right now is a tricky, maybe even dangerous question to have to fool around with. What can I possibly come up with. Oh, woe! This will have to do. "Are you in the book?"

"I am now. Thank you."

Pow! Now I know where I am. I'm in the flower garden that was once Claire Fullblood's. "And Claire and Certainly are sitting side by side at the smallish carved-oak table, looking through pale sheers out the five-panel, bay window at the colorful garden at the side of the house." I must have spent the night here among the blossoms and vines. Yow! That's not Claire nor Certainly Ridge looking out the window at me! I'd best be moving along. What was it that Mimi said about this house? "When Near died he willed it to some charitable institution. They're using it for their headquarters now."

"Jolty! Jolty Jone!"

The person from the window is rushing out the door. How come she knows my name? I'm brushing the vegetation off my backside. "Why do you know my name?"

The short, roundish woman with a sincere smile and reaching hands stops, thinks, answers. "I know your name because I am your friend. I have been helping you with your trip through life for quite some time now. You have found your way here many times before." She steps up to me and rests the palm of her hand on the point of my shoulder.

She's ribbin' me? No, she is definitely in earnest. Her hand on my shoulder is not unpleasant. I am thinking the optic nerves behind her eyes must be made of high-grade rubber. For she is a full head shorter than me, but our eyes are nearly touching! Her eyes are dark, very dark. The holes at the center of the eyeballs are not black. I can see into them. I see in there the light that fills all space yet shines on nothing.

"Remi Targ."

She meant for me to hear that as her name. I repeat it to myself. Remi Targ.

+

Claire was your mother.

What?

She died giving birth to you.

Many times before. Skads of times before.

The sign over the door of Mimi's café reads THE CLAIRE FULLBLOOD CAFE. And under that, in smaller letters, NEAR MOSS AND MIMI REAMS, PROPRIETORS.

Mimi never told Near Moss about my existence, and she told me flatly that she has never located Certainly Ridge. The primary difference lies in appearance, or, rather, in the lack of it. It does not appear that you and I are completely separate people, the way Jane and Rei are separate people. What does this/that have to do with Mimi Reams and her café and Near Moss and Certainly Ridge, you ask me. I am not certain yet. But I am working on the answer. So, please, excuse the apparently sloppy paragraphing.

"Jolty…you might want to get out of bed now."

That was Remi Targ calling me from another room, calling me, not TheRealJJ. I'm lying in Claire Fullblood's bed. (…in my mother's bed? I'll try to get back to that question later.) Remi offered me this room to use "for as long as you feel like staying here in the house."

Are the big painted scenes still up on the walls of the room with two bay windows? I can answer that question before I get out of bed. Yes. They're still there, just like all of Claire's bedroom furniture is still in here. Remy Targ has outfitted one of the other bedrooms as an office, but I think very little else in this house has been changed since Claire left it.

I went into that painted room last night just as the sun was going down and the ground fog was creeping in the windows. The scenes were at first breathtaking due to their size; then, after just a couple of minutes had passed with me slowly turning and staring at the walls, I found the quiet nostalgia of the scenes heartrending to the point of tears. And! I especially like Claire's most favorite painting, the small tropical painting that she and Certainly had left a wide unpainted band around. The figure in that painting who's starting to stand up is her, Claire. Yes, I recognized her. She *was* the woman under my death tree.

I also went out to look in the garage last night. In the dim I could just barely make out an old automobile covered with dust.

But before that, I remember now, I went out through the laundry room to sit on Claire's crying porch. It's a nice place to sit, on the stoop that is, my having already cried all that I was capable of (two meager tears) in the painted room notwithstanding.

Thirst is getting me up from this bed. Water! I yelled that to myself. Even so, Remi has a glass of H_2O in her hand waiting for me as I turn the corner into the kitchen. Is she hearing my thoughts? Do I have a conniption over my lack of privacy, sometimes called a conniption fit? Not at all. I had been, I realize, relating too strongly internally to the external. I'll just cut off that way of thinking completely again—I *had* become lax.

"Go ahead and sit down, Jolty. What are you eating nowadays? It was nothing but nettles and fresh rose petals for a while, wasn't it? How about some rolled oats? I've cooked some for us."

Having swallowed the water at one big draught, I'm no longer thirsty. I lie about the rolled oats. "They would be just fine, Remi." Because now I'm hungry. I haven't experienced hunger this big for longer than I can remember.

"I saw you walking by here one evening a while back." Remi carries a tray of food and eating ware to the table and sits herself down across from me. "You were in the company of your friend-of-old, Mimi Reams."

Whew! Everywhere I go, people know my name. Everywhere I go, people know everything I've been doing. Calm yourself, I tell myself. Just be nice. Just laugh falsely and say, "No comment at this time."

Remi's laugh is realer than mine. And more pleasing to my ears than mine. "You must be planning to go into politics, Jolt."

Jolt? Yep, that's what she called me. Am I *The Jolt*? Anything but serious am I when I reply, "Would you vote for me, The Jolt, if I did?"

"Sure. Why not? Is this enough in your bowl?"

"Enough for now, I always say. Hey?" Truly it's a big portion she's offering me.

"What should we do today, Jolt? Do you want to just relax alone or together here in the house? Or should we go somewhere? Or should we sit here at the table all day long discussing whatever comes up?"

I haven't had that many agreeable choices offered all at once for longer than I can remember. But I'm not going to pick one of them. Nope. "Could I go back to bed, Remi?"

"Of course you can." She seems happy with my request. "You can sleep the day away. I have plenty of other things to do."

How many days and nights did that three-headed guy in the fairy tales sleep? More than I will, for sure—but not by much!

Remi came in and actually tucked me into bed. We both laughed about that. Such a silly scene it was.

I'm rising sweetly above the bed. Then someone aims my identity at me, and I splatter so hard back down against the bed that I feel every bone in my body break. Doesn't that sound like a Claire Fullblood dream? I must be dreaming of her. In a part of my mind that I'm ignoring. Ignoring? I try to turn my body over. It's nothing but a bag of bone chips and dust.

She could not be finishing life at a worse time.

Did he say that she could not be finishing life at a worse time?

I ask him, She could not be finishing life at a worse time?

She could not be finishing life at a worse time.

How could one time be any different to die at than any other time? It seems to me that dying can only be timeless. But! Now I remember that old word-group: "…died a timely death." That *timely*, however, is timely only for those who are not ready yet to die, the survivors, if you will, not for the dier. Who is *he* and who is *she?* Just two eerie, personality-less inhabitants of my dream—of one of my many dreams today in Claire's bed.

Room…room…room. Still cocooned in a dream, the next dream, I get up and walk about the room. Yes, I am fully aware that I am dreaming. I am not ignoring, not now. The room looks pretty much the same, except it's nighttime now. Or it's as dark as nighttime in the room. Claire comes in the door. I immediately flatten myself against the wall. She approaches the bed, takes off her sheer nightgown, and crawls under the covers. She's soon asleep. Her eyelids are moving as if she's dreaming. I don't know what to do. Should I wait where I am until she gets up and comes over to me thinking I'm Certainly Ridge?

+

"TheRealJJ."

"That's one word?"

"Yes, one word with four caps."

Remi gets up from her chair and walks about the room, not Claire's bedroom, the bedroom that Remi had converted to an office. "So you think, Jolty, that the person who I think has come to stay with me a number of times before is not you but might be this TheRealJJ?"

She called me Jolty this time. "That is the possibility that occurs to me."

She returns to her chair. "You don't remember ever

coming here yourself?"

Her *ever* is a tricky word. So I won't answer her question. Then I decide that I will answer it. "I have had deep, accurate memories of the inside of this house *forever*, yet I have no memory of *ever* being inside of the house before."

"TheRealJJ, to use the name you coined, has changed many people's minds, has changed their minds forever for the good."

"For the good?"

"Most definitely for the good, Jolty."

"What about your mind, Remi?"

"My mind has been changed, too. I have learned from TheRealJJ and found peace."

To tell you the truth, this woman is starting to scare me. I think it is well on to time to get my lowly self out of here. "Whelp, guess I'll be going now."

"Do you have somewhere in particular to go, Jolty?"

"Nope, I'll just be moving on down the road." I have not yet stood up.

"Want some company?"

Now that is a strange question for her to ask me. I suddenly can't help stuttering. Stuttering is a friend of mine? "Wh-wh-wh-ere would we go?"

"Wherever you go, of course."

"I couldn't do that!"

"The Jolt can't do what?"

"I couldn't take someone with me."

"Why not?"

I hear myself asking that same question, thinking it is a good question.

+

Ding! Ding! Ring!

Ding! Ding! Ring!

I'm hearing something coming.

Aha! It's a gold and silver understanding. Except for
a few slippery wiggles that I will necessarily leave out
because I lack the (adequate) prearrangements of words to
describe them, my g&s understanding goes something like
this: Remi had to have had her office in ex-Claire's house
(and had to have had TheRealJJ visit her there "many
times") *before* Near Moss died and willed the house "to some
charitable institution," which just might mean that Near
Moss was quite aware of the existence of TheRealJJ, which
does not contradict Mimi's telling me (without the slightest
hint of ambiguity in her voice that I can recall) that she
never told Near Moss about me and that Near never once
laid his eyes on me. Still, it's possible that Near knew about
me anyway, even if he never once saw me.

Having thought more than enough-tough about
that, I will now think in depth about the light I saw inside
Remi's eyeballs that time—I have carefully avoided looking
squarely into Remi's eyes ever since. First I see that, yes, the
light is the same light I saw while I was under the water for
some time—either while I was under water or shortly
thereafter. Second, I see that for Remi to not even make a
mention to me of the light that lives inside her must be
extremely difficult for her. Does she think that if she talks
too readily about it she will not be able to sustain the light,
that it will go away?

Talk about tough-rough decisions, I did let her come with me. We don't get very far, though. We are side-by-siding down the sidewalk with the hereabouts looking very familiar to m—looking like the bare bottom of the universe again with that giant butt sticking up in the distance—when Remi tugs on my sleeve, pulling me into Mimi's café.

Mimi is not looking at me, not at all. Oh, she is ignoring me. No, she does not know me! She does too know me. She doesn't. She does.

It looks like Remi and I will have to sit here a good week before we get waited on. I glance nervously at Remi. She smiles peacefully back at me. Then Remi stands up and puts her hand out in front of her with its palm turned up as if she's testing for rain. She raises the hand...ah! It's to tell me to stand up, too. I do that. Quick as a well-trained dog, I am up on my two hind legs. (Do any sentient beings *normally* have more or less than two hindermost legs?) Remi spins like a round ballerina and takes the lead to the door, not looking back to check the effect our exit is having on Mimi. So I don't look back either.

"Bark!"

"What?" asks Remi when we are out again on the sidewalk.

"Bark! Bark!"

Remi's eyes begin to twinkle and her mouth turns up into a smile as she realizes why I barked. "No, Jolty. I have no interest in being your master. In the future I will make my gestures more obviously requests and not orders."

-20-

ACEHOR VINSBEL PECO

What I hear after looking up long at the Shoefoot's Shoe sign is Acehor Vinsbel Peco striding up the sidewalk toward me, dragging his giant gold finger ring on the black iron pickets of the fence. He be the man I be here to meet under this sign. How do I know that *this* man—a bright-eyed, salt-and-pepper man all geared up in a wide-woven unbuttoned brown jacket, a screaming pink shirt, razor-creased tan pants, shiny black pointed shoes—is Acehor Vinsbel Peco? In his free hand he bears a pole bearing a banner bearing his name. Directly under his name on the banner are two three-letter words, *You Bet*, followed by a bold exclamation point. Therefore I have no doubt about whom I am about to meet.

"Be you Jolty Jone?" The man spoke with six to twelve interesting accents all at the same time.

"That I am. I am not, however, TheRealJJ. So I may not be in fact the real Jolty Jone."

"You are a tease, aren't you. I like that." Acehor leans his banner and pole against the fence so that he can withdraw something from his shirt pocket. A small notepad. And a pen. "I'm writing down that word, *TheRealJJ*. It was just one word, wasn't it, one word with four capital letters? This is a word you made up yourself? I like it."

And I like Acehor. Remi said I would. (He just might make a woman out of me.) "Yes, one word, a one word name for who knows how many people."

"What's that you said? '...for who knows how many

people'? Was that merely a touch of your own special brand of humor, part of a wordy joke? Or were you hinting at some esoteric knowledge you possess? Or! There's always… Hmm. Statements like that are *always* potentially true, aren't they? Are you—to use a seriously dated saying—playing with my head?"

AVP obviously enjoys talking. Hence I don't hesitate before answering him. "Yes, I made up the word myself. But I don't count it among the major accomplishments of my life. It's schoolkid stuff."

"Quite. I quite agree. Schoolkid stuff. Really to the point it is, though, I must say." Acehor is shaking his head (as well as his tightly curled hair with its zebra patches of black and grey), and I see that he is stringing words in a shallow curve toward something difficult. "Tell me if you would, Jolty—is it all right if I call you Jolty, inasmuch as you did agree that you are Jolty Jone?" He barely gives me time to nod my head before delivering the difficulty. "Will you please tell me of these major accomplishments of your life?"

"I think you are wanting to talk to TheRealJJ, Acehor."

That was a miserly response, I tell myself. Any comeback like *that* will be grossly insufficient to divert this man from his question.

So I take the next evasive tactic that occurs to me. "Is it all right if I call you Acehor, inasmuch as you approached me with your name streaming in the air above your head? Or are you instead *You Bet* being trailed by 'a period that blew its top'?"

"You may call me either Acehor or AV."

"Not AVP?"

"That's a bit much, don't you think?"

Droll he is.

So I tell him right back with the force in my voice of a fourth-grade schoolteacher making a trivial point emphatically clear to the class, "What's a bit much is the sign above our heads," speaking, of course, of the red and black Shoefoot's Shoe sign.

Acehor nearly stumbles backward when he looks up at the sign. Had he not even noticed it was there? Or was he knocked back by the words on the sign? I guess that puts me one-up on him. But, no, Acehor is quick. "Was that your strong *inside* voice or your strong *outside* voice? And as to the sign, Jolty, that's but another way of saying, 'Horses are the answer to it all.' Some time ago, shortly after the appearance of that sign, I went and found the man who put it up there and inquired its meaning. The man's brain was a horseshoe."

My diversion appears to have worked. "You reside in this area then, AV?"

"Yes, yes, yes. I'm right over there." He raises his shoulders and points that great ring finger at a magnificent old two-story, handbuilt building across the street. "But you must not lead me away from my question without notifying me first that you intend to. Honesty is productive, both mutually and individually. Sneakiness is not productive. Sneakiness deceives only the deceiver."

"Am I being scolded, Acehor?"

"Yes!"

I haven't seen *that* look—the look that takes Acehor's face—for what must be a long time: a thin concave bottle of pale purple glass that is about to break. His face does not break but melts into a sweet candor. "To be completely honest, Jolty, it is also my way of turning the tables on you."

"Well," I admit, "seeing as the tables are well turned by now, I will answer your question. The answer is no."

Acehor harrumphs. And waits.

"No, I repeat. I will not tell you because I have accomplished exactly nothing. Or, if that's not true, whatever I have accomplished is spread so thin over time and space that it is as good as invisible. As good as gone. As invisible as time and space."

"I cannot tell from your tone, Jolty, but your words do seem to be soliciting pity."

"And I think *you* are rushing to push me into completely unfamiliar territory, Acehor. Pity indeed!"

"Would you know if self-pity is unfamiliar territory for you?"

"That's an interesting question. I will consider it. Yet from where I'm standing right now I will have to say, 'Of course I would!'"

"You don't have an inside voice, do you?"

"Probably not."

"Why did our lovely Remi Targ arrange for you and me to meet? I have been especially curious to know this ever since you told me that you may not be in fact the real Jolty Jone."

"What's that you said? 'Our lovely Remi Targ'? You have a strange way of talking, Acehor. Your choice of words, that is. Is what catches my attention a time question or a style question? And the sounds of your words too!

How do you say the words so many different ways at once?"

"Both my words and the sounds of my words, you ask." Acehor pulls on his chin. "They must be totally both time and style. Time and style *lived*, I would say, roughly equals time and style *borrowed*."

I'm talking rather strangely, too, aren't I. It must be the company I'm in. How could anyone not be attracted to a magnet as strong as Acehor's? "We might find out whether I have an inside voice if we stroll over and into your home over there," say I with dead calm while pointing my un-finger-ring-ed ring finger at the building.

"Sure, sure, sure." Acehor glances this way and that. "Never liked standing under this sign anyway. You lead the way."

"Now don't forget your pole banner."

"Ah. I probably would have. Thank you."

We are a two-piece parade crossing the street, swinging way wide to the right to make a left turn that we don't make.

We are across the street. We are up on the front porch. There is a cloud of clothed flesh (sitting?) on a wood rocker next to the door. Acehor is reaching for the doorknob. The nebulous, faceless person says, to me I think, "Life's a series of deep dips separated by high plains, short stretches of high plain, so that every time I come up onto a plain it's 'Hey! It's a bright shiny new world!' But I soon drop into another, uh, dip, and it's 'Here I am again.' Which is why it is of primary concern to most people most of the time that their presence is acknowledged."

Acehor is watching my face to catch my reaction. It

is easy for me to show no reaction whatsoever. Seemingly satisfied with my deadpan, Acehor instructs me, "Don't say anything; it will be the wrong thing to have said. Just nod your head silently in acknowledgment."

I do that.

(Everything was going on like that until I found my death-tree again. I climbed up in it and died, of course, having known or figured out that wanting to be gone is, uh, one thing, but actually learning how to turn off the machine is quite another thing. The machine *does* turn off. Goodbye.)

Acehor and I are inside the building and have closed the door behind us. AV whispers to my ear, "Haze can destroy the heritage of a house—or of any place, for that matter—in a matter of moments. In a matter of moments, everything is exactly right here, exactly right now. That's his talent and his work. All you need to do to get on with him is to let him know that you are aware he is there."

"How do you know that Haze is a *he*, Acehor?"

AV grins at me with undisguised guile. "A much used line from popular literature, Jolty, says, 'That is one of my secrets that you will never know.'"

The bottom floor of the large building/house is open for use to all three of the residents and their guests, AV explains to me as we climb the stairs to the second floor, which, I'm told, is divided into three multi-room apartments. Everything is dark, polished wood and fine carpet.

"That door is Haze's. Down there is Mike's door. And this one is mine."

Did he say *Mack's* door? No. He said "Mike's."

We are inside Acehor's apartment now, and it's just

lovely, a dream. What a place to live! There is nothing, not a single ostentatious thing in the apartment; no, everything is just a little bit better made than anything similar that I've seen (recently?). I quickly pull off my clothes and go in search of the bathtub.

I have found the tub and filled the tub and have been soaking my tired body back to freshness long enough that I can feel the hot water starting to do its (humorous?) work. The door opens and naked Acehor, without the slightest pomp, joins me. Take my word for it, he is a man. Yah! He slides into the tub facing me.

No. I'm keeping my eye on the door, but the mysterious third resident of the place, Mike, has not so far all of a sudden ambled into the bathroom for a howdy. Nor has the blob, who maybe can't amble anyway.

Conversing with each other joyfully and exuberantly about deeply insignificant matters, Acehor and I turn one at a time in the tub to have our backs washed by the other, both of us laughing a lot with our mouths open. What a life! Particularly since I'm dead.

Dead or alive, I make a request. "Give me another quote from popular literature, AV. Please."

"OK. This is from The Fourth Cactus, Jolty. 'When you are ten feet under water in a swimming pool, you do certain things for your pleasure and certain things for your survival. As long as you remain under the water, it does not matter a whole bunch to you what town the pool is in.' OK?"

"Whew! You remember stuff like that?"

"As if the words are divine, yes."

"That's uncomfortable—no, that's confusing for me

to think about, Acehor. Shoot a request at me."

"Where were you born?"

"I don't know exactly." I shake my head severely. "Somewhere hereabouts? I think I've been told that."

"When were you born, Jolty?"

"I don't rightly remember that either, AV."

"Were you in fact born, Jolty?"

Oops, that calls for an immediate splashing of soapy water at his face. Followed by a lot more shared laughter.

Acehor's still laughing when he inquires, "Would you accept a place and a time of your birth, Jolty, if someone told you them?"

"Who would tell me? You?"

"No, not me. You will have to tell me who."

"Doesn't that make your question circular, AV?"

"Not necessarily, Jolty. There is a *straight and narrow* way of approaching my question with the condition tacked onto it."

"I thought we were bathing."

"We *are* bathing."

"It doesn't sound like bathing any longer, AV."

"Shall we climb out then?"

We are out, out of the tub, standing on a white mat, drying each other's backs with plush towels, discussing what to have for dinner, laughing a little less nervously, when the building blows up.

Acehor and I are now billions of smithereens flying through the universe in search of rebirth. We are heading in every which direction; so we don't talk to each other.

Of course the building didn't blow up. I blew up. After what Acehor did to me next, *physically* speaking, I blew up and away forever. "Thank you, Acehor Vinsbel Peco."

"And I thank you, Jolty Jone. Thank you. Thank you."

I am no longer a salamander on Mars.

+

I'm thinking I should have said *jellyfish* instead of *salamander*. I looked up the term *sex* in an ancient, crumbling encyclopedia that I found this morning in Acehor's library. I'm understanding now that the way I used to see myself (before Acehor straightened me out) was more like I was a lone jellyfish down as deep as I could get in the dark and dense aqua of a northern sound. As an *individual* jellyfish I could never quite make out the powerful ferryboats of males and females passing overhead. *C'est la vie!* (Right. I uncovered that "famously foreign" phrase in the friendly library, too.)

A boyishly handsome man just knocked on the front door and is being let in to the apartment by Acehor. I use the six seconds that it takes the man to cross the room from Acehor to where I'm standing in the kitchen doorway; I use the time to observe him. The man is pretending. Definitely pretending. But is this man pretending to be a gentle, retiring type or pretending to be always cool and reserved around people he doesn't know or hasn't accepted yet? I will soon find out.

The man takes my hand in his soft hands, yet he doesn't speak to me. He merely smiles liquidly at my eyes and silently nods his head in acknowledgment of my presence.

"He hasn't spoken a word since he moved into this house," says Acehor from across the room. "But you can talk to him if you like. You might keep in mind, though, that he sees uncommonly deep into you and your words."

I decide to respect the man's silence with a silver silence of my own. I mirror the nod of his head. He lets go of my hand and walks briskly to the picture window that looks out across the street. (At the Shoefoot's Shoe sign?) I walk over and stand beside him. He does appear to be staring at the sign. Quick as a metal switch, the man turns and leaves the apartment, giving Acehor the high sign on the way out.

When Acehor has closed the door, I immediately ask him, "What was that?"

"That was Mike."

+

"Do you mean the Mike who is one of your two neighbors?"

"Yes. He is the mum one of my two neighbors."

"How do you know that this easy-to-look-at neighbor of yours sees deep into people and what they say, Acehor?"

"That be another of my secrets that you will never know, my Jolty. You have probably seen Mike for the last time."

"He's going somewhere?"

"No. He isn't going anywhere as far as I know."

"Oh." I swishswash my tail over the floor to lean against the closed door beside Acehor. "What about Haze?

Will I see him again?"

"Probably not, Jolty, if you continue to pay attention at the level that you are now. One meeting is usually enough then. If you get too self-absorbed, though, you two will undoubtedly meet over and over again."

I have to laugh at that. "He will be the thermometer of my awareness."

+

To use a *more* seriously dated saying, I took an unexpected turn for the worse and Haze and I are meeting a couple of times a day and a couple of times a night. This guy—I'm taking Acehor's word for it that Haze is male, and human—can really bring me right down flat on the ground. Everytime I start howling at the moon, bang, there he is reminding me that I'm not a wolf. Speaking of the moon… Yes, the closest I can get to a description of what Haze looks like in the daylight is to call him a featureless raincloud. Yet at night he is that fuzzy-man-in-the-moon. He doesn't have the righteous glow of the moon that's in the sky, but Haze *almost* has a face at night.

No sight or sign of Mike. Haven't seen him since that first time. I'm kind of glad about that, though. I don't know what I could say to him.

No matter. I've got Acehor to talk to. We lay in bed talking; we sit out in his sunny living room chatting for hours; we walk all over town discussing this and that, completely oblivious of everyone else in the world. And the longer and longer it is that we are seeing each other, the realer I feel. But! But! But! The more that Acehor and I talk and the realer that I get, the more limited I feel. Definitely. More limited. That's what I would call a *fact*.

Haze is not a fact. I don't think Haze actually exists, at least not in the way that I am seeing him. He's probably just a normal looking and normal acting person who I am viewing through the remaining filters of my last past life—if anything around Acehor Vinsbel Peco can be considered normal. Tomorrow morning I just might wake up and see that Haze has one of those *beautiful* faces up on the info-boards.

I think I have dreamed something that's similar to this wrong-viewing of Haze. Let me try to remember. Yes. *I am aware that all these planets are composed in my mind…while on still another planet, an amorphous cloud high in the sky is the one and only source of light.* Is that what I'm thinking of? Is that the dream I'm trying to remember? Is Haze the light shining in from outside my made-up world?

A world without light is at least imaginable, at least temporarily imaginable. But a world without words? A world that's maybe like the one Mike occupies? Nope! I can't even imagine a world like that. So Mike too must be a dream partially remembered.

Aggh! No dream of wordlessness comes to mind. There must be one such dream *somewhere*! I cast everywhere in the sea of my personal memory. Alas.

It's readily apparent at this moment that I am tethered to my world by words and only by words. If there be any means other than words to remain worldly, I'm just not seeing it. Perhaps what AV and his neighbors are doing for me is showing me another way. Sitting up straightbacked in this straightback chair, staring again at the ceiling, gazing one more time at the speckled kitchen ceiling, thinking about the way AV dresses and the way he speaks, thinking about the magic hidden in his method of clothing himself, in his multiple accents, I ever so quickly glimpse the other side, from whence I came. And in the next instant I realize that the object is not to *get* up the hill but to *go* up the hill. Doing. No one need look any farther for the engine of life. I roll the word *doing* around and round in my brain. Then— yike!—I hear in my head the high-pitched voice of a very young person. "I saw them doing it! I did! I did!" I remember the voice clearly but cannot remember whose voice it is. I think it must have been the voice of somone whom I was a buddy to way way long time ago. Was it Mimi's voice? I still dream of lying beside Mimi in her bed. In my dreams she has shaved her head again yet has not painted herself green. Certainly Ridge once stood over the bed gazing down at Claire Fullblood. I climb to my feet and gaze down at Mimi Reams. I too see a silver coin at the bottom of our pond.

SOME OF THAT MIDDLE HORN

Acehor is telling me how I look cutely slightly-embarrassed most all of the time whenever there is someone else in our midst.

So I defend myself. "You silly boy. I am just easily entertained."

Yet he comes back instantly. "And you deftly control the click of your heels."

This is crazy! So I throw the discussion into the absurd. "But only when I'm wearing a red bandanna in my hair. Or when I'm napping on the sofa sometimes. You may have noticed that."

We are standing together near the picture window. AV's watching a pair of snappy white shoes walking by outside the window. "No, I can't say that I have, Jolty."

I'm looking across the room and through the door into Acehor's office. "Did I see a new stack of papers on your desk a while ago, Acehor?"

"You might have. It's a manuscript sent to me by Iiu Sxpeed."

"What's the ms about?"

"Stripped beings."

"Beings stripped of what?"

"In the eyes of Iiu Sxpeed, Jolty, there seems to be a growing number of humans—and I dare say he includes the members of a number of other species too—who are missing many of the aspects of personality that *we* have always considered fundamental."

"Oooh! You're trying to scare me now!" I cover the top of my head with my forearms.

Before AV can wittily (or fittingly) reply, I rise up onto my tiptoes and dance around the room with my arms still sheltering my head and my hands flapping the air like wings.

"Have no fear: the manuscript is not about you, Jolty. Iiu Sxpeed most likely has never even heard of you or of your famous book. Iiu Sxpeed lives in a world that famous things cannot reach, a world probably not all that different from the world you yourself were inhabiting immediately before Remi Targ found you this last time."

Remi Targ found *me*? Now is not the time to argue about such trivialities, I tell myself; let us face instead this "famous book" issue.

I cannot see, feel, or taste how Acehor could be referring to any other book than the book on Mimi's bedtable: *DODOWN DOUP: A Non-Agreed Upon Vision of the World*, by Jolty Jone. But for Acehor to speak of that book as mine doesn't make a whole bunch of sense to me, since I have firmly established that book as having been written by TheRealJJ and I have firmly stated to Acehor Vinsbel Peco that I am not TheRealJJ. Which probably means... Which probably means that Acehor (and maybe Remi Targ too) think I'm TheRealJJ.

How can I prove to them I'm not? I've never actually *seen* TheRealJJ; have they? Are AV and Remi trying to form two or more people into one? Or are they trying to form two or more people from one? All these are good questions, I'm sure. But what is the root question?

"I would start with the question of how individuals

are identified." Yes, that was me talking. I said that out loud to Acehor.

"What?" Acehor looks stunned. Then he smiles directly at my eyes. "Are you planning to write another book, Jolty?"

Maybe *stunned* was too strong of a word. Yes, I'm sure it was. Before Acehor looks stunned, the world will have to be literally coming apart.

Play it dumb, kid.

OK. What would sound dumb?

Try this: Another book? What, pray tell, are you talking about, AV?

That sounded pretty dumb to me.

"Another book? What, pray tell, AV, are you talking about?"

Acehor grins knowingly. "Playing it dumb, huh, kid?"

He's so sharp sometimes. —Or is this the first time he has let on that he hears my thoughts? Hmm. No, I don't think he's that kind of reader; he is not like Jane and Rei. I think he is extremely aware of everything that is going on around him...and he remembers it all... and he moves easily back and forth between me and this great memory bank of his. But I will monitor our future conversations more closely.

-PART 2-
YOO-HOO—WE'RE BACK

As you can see, I bailed out of that wreck just before it *totally* crashed. No? You don't see that? Which wreck am I talking about, you ask? The last time that you and I were together with Acehor Vinsbel Peco, he asked me, "Are you planning to write another book?" Mucho time has passed and Acehor's out of my life, but I'll answer his question now: yes. You just read it. Yes, that (ugly) train of chapters numbered 1 through 21 *is* the book. Its homely little title, *dodown*, is obviously a bald-faced rip-off of the title of my first book, *DODOWN DOUP: A Non-Agreed Upon Vision of the World*. As you are certainly aware now that you've read it, *dodown* is not in any way grand. Like its simple-minded, pared down title, it's "not much for looks at all," if you can tolerate such a horrid understatement. So, no matter how long it is *out there*, it will never be even as successful as *DODOWN DOUP ETC* was in it's very first month. Hey, perhaps you've figured out by now that I jumped off that wreck—the utterly dippy *dodown* train— right into the arms of Jane Hupiter and Rei Reus. In the short while that I stayed with Acehor, I realized/remembered many things. For example, I can never return to bed&work with Mimi because she believes in only one of my two primary ingredients: our precious Mimi Reams and TheRealJJ live in well separated worlds. (A caveat: In spite of all my new understandings, I am still quite unsure of my real relationship to Zole of Zole&Felix. Oh well.) Yes. I am Jolty Jone. Yes, I am also TheRealJJ.

The split between *Jolty Jone* and *TheRealJJ* was never as deep, cheap and nasty as chapters 19-21 of *dodown* made it sound. The two J's re-merged (in a way) and are happily (in a way) coexisting, though they do forever face in opposite directions. Still there be nothing to prevent them from slowly drifting apart again. Of the two *J's*, the factor that *your Jolty* referred to in your presence (in chapter 19) as "the bodiless voice" before designating it "TheRealJJ"—that factor is at this time, right now the apparent dominate of the two. Perhaps you can hear a slight change of voice. Actually, obviously, both of these J-factors must be taken together to see the one true Jolty Jone. —Excuse me for a moment, please; I think I just heard a knock at the door downstairs.

Then you hear me climbing down the stairs and striding across the lower floor to the door. After a few seconds of silence, you hear the muffled sound of me saying, "If you absolutely must come in…"

www.ingramcontent.com/pod-product-compliance
Lightning Source LLC
Chambersburg PA
CBHW031123030726
47496CB00002BA/659